DEATH'S OBSESSION

AVINA ST. GRAVES

Death's Obsession by Avina St. Graves

Published by Avina St. Graves

Contact the author at avina.stgraves@gmail.com

Copyright © 2023 Avina St. Graves

Cover by Beholden Cover
Chapter Header/photo by Mitja Juraja
Skull by Nika Rybczynska
Formatting made with Atticus

ISBN 978-0-473-68084-8
First Edition

TRIGGERS

This book is considered dark and mature. It is not suitable for people under the age of 18. Triggers include (but are not limited to):

Stalking, death, dubcon, anal, double penetration, impact play, breath control, mental illness, emotionally and physically abusive romantic relationship (not with MMC), prescription drug use, alcohol and drug abuse, sibling death, parent death, cancer (off screen), PTSD, depression, anxiety, hallucinations, dissociation, traumatic events, suicidal ideation, attempted suicide (off screen), recording of sexual intercourse without consent, depiction of a violent car crash.

AUTHOR'S NOTE

IF YOU BY CHANCE know Greek mythology and are well versed in Latin, I sincerely apologize for this book. It won't be accurate.

PLAYLIST

Death's Obsession on Spotify, as curated by my biggest fan, V:

It's Called: Freefall – Rainbow Kitten Surprise

Snow White Queen – Evanescence

Find You – Ruelle

Moondust (Stripped) – Jaymes Young

Afterlife – Nothing But Thieves

The Other Side – Ruelle

Fear of the Water – SYML

No Time To Die – Billie Eilish

I Found – Amber Run

Flawless – The Neighbourhood

Heavenly – Cigarettes After Sex

Mr. Sandman – SYML

Terrible Thing – AG

Paint It, Black – Ciara

Gods & Monsters – Lana Del Rey

Broken – Lund

Spiracle – Flower Face

After Dark – Mr.Kitty

DEDICATION

To the girls who think that the grim reaper will fuck like a god.

MEMENTO MORI

REMEMBER YOU MUST DIE

PROLOGUE

Birth. Life. Death.

Heaven. Hell. Purgatory.

Good or bad, I will find you. You will not escape me. For I am *he*. For I am *it*.

You will run. They all run. You run thinking I will never catch you. You run thinking if you hide well enough, I will never find you.

You pray to your god I will never take you. You beg I never find the ones you love. Each plea falls on deaf ears, because I am coming.

You may think I will chase you to the end of the earth on my chariot, press my lips to yours and let your body rest peacefully. Even when you come willingly, you scream and fight for life. Praying and pleading that it is not your time, that you have more to do, more to accomplish. You claim to need more years under the sun, but you will never be ready. For what is death, in the face of life?

You claim I want your soul, that your death is only in my hands. But I do not want it. Your soul is yours to keep until it is not.

I have never wanted a soul until her.

My Lilith. My night monster.

She is a storm on winter's day, and I will be content with never seeing the sun again.

She offered me her soul, and I gave it back. Not because I did not want it. *Oh,* I wanted it like a flower wants the sun, like a river wants the sea. When I come to collect her soul, it will not be to take her to the afterlife. No, her soul will be mine to keep.

CHAPTER ONE

LILITH

You look beautiful when you sleep.

I READ THE NOTE again, over and over. *I'm not crazy. The letter is real.*

The harsh glow of moonlight only just makes the words more visible. I have to hold the thick brown parchment with both hands to stop it from curling back together. Each swirl of black ink is another coil that winds tighter around my stomach. The letters taper at each end, as if it was written with a fountain pen.

He was here again. He was watching me sleep.

I wrote the note in my sleep, I tell myself, just like Dr. Mallory told me to.

It doesn't matter how many times I say it or scream it into my pillow or write it down, I don't believe my own words. The letters are real. I know they are, even though no one else believes me.

I told Dr. Mallory about the man who visited me on the day of the accident, face hidden under the shadows of his hood. Then the gifts started appearing. Then the letters. Then came the symbols. All from him. *The Faceless Man.*

I tried showing Dr. Mallory that the letters are real, that I'm not hallucinating like she claims. In fact, I tried to prove to everyone that someone was watching me and leaving me letters. No one believed me—they think it's just the ramblings of a woman gone mad. I'd take pictures of the letters, only for them to disappear from my phone. Every time I put the letters in my bag, they become lost to the void, only to appear back in my bedroom with a note that says:

It's our little secret.

I'm not crazy. I'm *not.*

The gifts he leaves are real. So are the symbols he draws on my body. I know they are.

"You bought yourself flowers, Lili, you just forgot about it," Dr. Mallory said, even though I've never been fond of flowers. When I told her about the symbols, she explained, *"You must have been sleepwalking and drew them on yourself."*

I thought she was right, because the man never visited when I stayed with Evan, either at his place or mine. I used to wake up in the morning or in the dead of the night with Evan by my side, and my body would be free from the marks the Faceless Man would leave. There would be no letters left on my pillow or on my bedside table. No flower atop my chest or my dresser. I'd be free from the nightmares of the Faceless Man, if only for a night. Although, I'm not sure if he is a nightmare or the sweetest of dreams.

Evan was my shield against the Faceless Man.

Until my stalker stopped caring about Evan's presence.

Evan's snore is the only sound to be heard in the small space of my room. It's too early for the dog upstairs to start barking or for the kids downstairs to start watching their shows before school. All the neighbors say that, at night, I'm the only sound in the complex, wailing or whimpering when the night terrors hit. Evan says I don't always have nightmares; sometimes I just talk in my sleep, but I don't always remember what the dreams are about. The only dreams I do remember are of the accident, and that's when the screaming starts.

That's why Evan prefers that we live separately, because he needs to 'stay sharp' for his job. He says he can't do that if I wake him from his sleep with my 'ramblings.'

When I lay next to Evan once a week, I try not to sleep, worried I'll wake him. I try so hard to stay awake, I swear I do. But Dr. Mallory's medication always puts me to sleep, even for just a few hours.

Inching the blankets down my bare legs, I creep across the room, not daring to look down at my body until the wooden panels beneath my feet turn to cold tile and the dull luminescent light of the bathroom glares down on me. Slowly, my eyes drop from my disheveled dark brown hair, down to the symbol painted on my chest and the black hand prints around my ample thighs, not hidden under my singlet and shorts. I can't see the twenty-centimeter scar along my stomach, or any of the other scars covering my body from the accident, but I know they're there.

I bite my tongue to stifle a sob and tear my gaze away from the mirror. Unfurling my fingers from around the note, I see the letter under the dull light and foolishly hope no words will look back at me. But as always, the cursive words taunt me: *You look beautiful when you sleep.*

I'm not sure which is more foolish: The fact that I'm hoping I'll find the words missing, or the fact that I hope the letters never stop.

Squeezing my eyes shut. I reach for a washcloth, not waiting for the water to warm before soaking the black fabric. I drop the letter on the vanity and distract myself with my own reflection. I can't help but touch the marks he left behind on my thighs. The mark left behind is far larger than my own hands, which is just more proof that I'm not crazy. I've stopped trying to convince people I'm not insane, but it's vindicating to have physical proof.

Used to cleaning the charcoal marks from my skin, I'm back in my room before much time passes and sliding open the drawer holding almost everything the Faceless Man has ever given me. The letter lands on top of one of the shoe boxes filled with the hundreds of notes he's left me. It's next to the pile of black bird feathers and the skulls of various animals.

I can't bring myself to throw any of them away, as some kind of tangible proof that I have not lost all of my sanity. Well, at least I tell myself that's the real reason why.

I've given up collecting the flowers he leaves me as they rot in a manner of days. All except one. My attention darts to the stemless lily sitting in the corner of the drawer, still full of life even after a year and a half of living in the cold prison of a wooden drawer. It's a coffin, just with less space.

With a shaky breath, I push the drawer full of the Faceless Man's gifts back into the darkness and slip between the cold sheets to lie next to a man who doesn't know those letters are the only reason I'm alive.

I wish I had died that day.

My mind darkens into nothing but white noise as the clock ticks by. Minute after minute. Hour after hour. It all passes in a blink while I'm safe in the comfort of my own mind. Until eventually, the clock beeps.

I died that day, but my body lived on. I can stare into space for hours, watching shadows stretch across a room and shrink back into the corner, without a thought in my mind or an emotion stirring in my chest. Sometimes I don't know if it's better to feel nothing at all or everything.

Time keeps ticking until I find another brown parchment in my hand. They make me feel like I have a heart, whether they make it flutter or thunder, I feel alive.

I wonder what you taste like, my dark storm.

Your whimpers are like a symphony of angels. What will your screams sound like?

Lilith, my night monster, my perfect other, soon, you will be all mine.

"Turn that thing off," Evan groans.

I blink, finally registering that the alarm has been blaring for over a minute already. Hitting the 'end' button, I mutter, "Sorry."

"It's like you're trying to give me a headache."

I swallow, and wait for the bed to dip and hear the shower start before pulling myself from the pillow to stare at the teddy bear sitting on top of my drawers. Its beady black eyes are trained on me as I pull out my phone and rewind through the nanny cam recording.

As always, the screen flickers, hours of recording disappearing along with any trace of what might have happened: whether the Faceless Man came into my room or if I really did walk the halls and leave myself notes, blissfully ignorant to reality.

The shower stops and the telltale sign of the curtains being drawn pulls me from my phone. I don't know why I bother checking anymore. I never find anything.

As soon as I step into the bathroom, I grit my teeth and glare at the puddle of water saturating my socks. "Can you please use the bath mat," I call out to Evan, knowing he can hear me past the ticking of the gas stove turning on.

An exacerbated sigh comes from the kitchen. "Jesus, Lili. It's too early in the morning for you to start an argument. It was obviously an accident."

I bite my tongue and swallow whatever retort would have never made it past my lips, and step into the shower only to wince when nothing but cold streams out. After four years, I know better than to say something back, even though he never used to be like this.

I close my eyes and let the cold bite my skin. At least it makes me feel something, even for just a little while. Evan stuck by me after the accident and stayed when I made claims about seeing the Faceless Man.

He didn't need to stay around or stand by me, but he did. I'm not sure how much longer I can keep holding my breath around him. I just know that I can't bring myself to say the words that would tear us apart.

"*Soon, my love.*" The baritone whisper chills me more than the water. I snap my eyes open and suck in a sharp breath from the dark shape just beyond the curtain.

He's here. The Faceless Man is here.

Gripping the plastic material, I yank it back expecting to see Evan or the Faceless Man. Instead, I'm greeted by my empty bathroom and the puddles of water on the tile floor.

Tugging the threadbare towel off the rail, I dry myself and slip into my work clothes as quickly as I can. I pause. My black jeans feel tighter than normal. It probably shrunk in the washing machine. It has been happening a lot lately, my clothes fitting differently.

The onslaught of thoughts about the Faceless Man pushes the mundane issue out of my head. I can't seriously be thinking about my clothes when my stalker might have been standing on the other side of the curtain while I showered.

I rush to the kitchen, as fast as my feet will carry me without alerting Evan to my disheveled state. My body thrums with nerves and pent-up *need*—need for what, I don't know. It doesn't feel like I can breathe until the familiar flimsy plastic bottle is in my hand and Dr. Mallory's white tablet is being washed down with water.

The sidewalk on the other side of the street is visible from this spot in the kitchen and so are the apartments directly across from me. I can't count how many times I've fought the urge to knock on their doors to ask if they saw the Faceless Man in my room.

I won't bother asking Evan if he saw the man, or if he heard him whisper those three words. The answer will be a solid no.

"Is this all?"

I lower the glass of water onto the table and turn to Evan. "What?"

Just say it, Lili. Just say those five words: I'm breaking up with you.

He holds up my black wallet, with the PU edges peeling and the threads fraying. "Are these all the tips that you made?"

Just say it, I think to myself. "I had to see Dr. Mallory." *Damn it, Lili.* I cringe inwardly. *Come on. You know that he's dragging you down. You've been meaning to say those five words for months now and you still haven't.*

He sighs and rakes his hand through his sodden gold hair. The soft morning light filters through the window, washing his face in an ashen glow. When did he start looking so depleted? He used to be so beautiful, so full of life and love, always insisting we go on adventures and drive up and down the coast, camping out in the back of his truck. Until I became too scared of driving out of the city. Though I was never really happy with that life; it always felt like something was wrong or missing.

Say it.

He sighs disappointedly. "I told you that they're dropping my hours and that you need to make more tips."

I frown. "I'm a barista, Evan, not a waitress. I stand behind a machine and make coffee, there's not much I can—"

"Maybe you should try a little harder." He throws up his hand. "It doesn't hurt to maybe smile more or actually talk to the customers. It isn't their fault that you haven't given them a reason to tip you more."

I lower my voice to dampen any emotions before they overflow. "I needed to see Dr. Mallory."

Dr. Mallory. Medication. Rent. All the reasons that meant that I never had more than a loaf of bread and a packet of pasta in my cupboard and powdered milk in my fridge because it works out cheaper than the real thing.

Evan and I used to cook all sorts of fancy meals with each other, back when we had money and a life. I liked making the food, and he liked eating it while I was still preparing the meal. My sister, Dahlia, used to call us a power couple.

"What about *my* needs, Lili?" He shakes his head. "Didn't you think about *me* before you went to see her? I told you that money is tight, and you go waste it on a shrink that *clearly* isn't helping very much."

"I thought—" I shut my mouth before I dig my grave deeper.

I was at the grocery store when I thought the Faceless Man was standing behind me, pulling my hair off my shoulder to breathe in my scent. I felt the tenor of his breath on my neck as he whispered, *"You smell divine, my midnight storm."*

His chest was against my back, but I was frozen with the thought that it was finally time to face my demon. When I finally gathered the courage to turn, the only other person down the aisle was an old woman peering at her shopping list. Except out of the corner of my eyes, I *swore* I saw Dahlia bloodied and bruised. Just like that, the Faceless Man was less frightening.

Maybe she's telling me that it's time to face my fears and visit her and my parents at Millyard Cemetery. But I can't bring myself to do it. Not yet. Maybe not ever.

I could tell Evan exactly why I needed to see Dr. Mallory, but he'd call me crazy. Like he always does. The two times I showed him the charcoal marks on my body, he called me "fucked in the head". Then he muttered something along the lines of me being the problem, not the medication.

Just say the five words. I'm. Breaking. Up. With. You.

"You're so selfish sometimes, Lili. How many times do I need to remind you that you aren't the only one who has needs," Evan scolds. I look away from him as tears burn my eyes and threaten to fall. But I know they won't fall, they never do.

Evan has done so much for me already; he stuck around and made sure that I didn't drown myself after I lost Dahlia in the accident. Well at least, when I did drown, that death didn't take me. So maybe I didn't really owe him anything.

Evan latches onto my arm and turns me to face him. "Don't you turn away from me when I'm speaking to you."

His fingers dig into my skin hard enough to leave a bruise. "You're hurting me," I gasp as I yank myself out of his grasp.

His eyes widen, and I take a step back as he reaches for me once more, circling his fingers around the same tender place. He pulls me to his chest, flattening his hand down my back and peppering half-hearted kisses to the top of my head. "I'm sorry baby. I didn't mean to. You know how I get in the morning when I haven't had my hit."

Three slow, ominous knocks shake the walls of my small apartment and we both tense.

"What was that?" Evan pulls away. "Did you hear that?" He moves to the front door and checks outside. No one will be there. Because *he* is outside, standing on the sidewalk, looking straight at me.

The Faceless Man.

Sometimes he wears a hoodie, sometimes he wears a cloak, sometimes he wears a cashmere coat. Every time, his hood is drawn over his head, shrouding his face in shadows. Even though I can't see his eyes, I know that he can see my soul. I'm waiting for the day that he takes it.

CHAPTER TWO

LILITH

I BLINK AND THE space where the Faceless Man once stood is empty. I dig the heel of my palm into my eyes and consider taking another one of the pills. They're meant to stop the hallucinations, but they've done nothing of the sort.

My phone chimes from my bedroom. I ignore Evan's frustrated rambles about people knocking on doors at seven in the morning and how now he doesn't have enough cash to top up his stash. I let my brain go numb and my feet lead me to where my phone is left lying in the center of the bed.

My brows knit together at the unknown number staring back at me. I unlock my phone to read the message. Chills rain over my body and I throw it back onto the bed.

No.

He communicates in letters, not texts. It can't be him. When did the Faceless Man adopt modern technology? This could be the proof that I need, a message on my phone showing that he's been watching me this whole time. That I didn't make this all up.

I take another fortifying breath and pick up my phone. Squeezing my eyes shut, I count to three and tell myself that I'm not imagining things before opening them again. The text is still there, sitting in a grey bubble in my inbox.

> **Unknown Sender:** Death comes in shadows in the light; it does not need to wait for the dark. For him, I will come as a hurricane.

No matter how many times I read the message, I can't make sense of it. Why must it be so cryptic? Without really thinking it through, I send a response:

> **Me:** Who are you?

I stare at the message thread, waiting for a response, but nothing comes. It was a stupid idea anyway. This whole situation is entirely one-sided, he talks to me and taunts me but doesn't want to hear what I say.

I nearly jump out of my skin when the phone chimes again. Honestly, I didn't expect him to respond. Mustering all my emotional energy, I read the message.

> **Unknown Sender:** You know me as well as I know you.

What on earth does he mean? My fingers fly across the keyboard, stringing together words to let him know just how sick I am of his games while in the back of my mind, I am hoping he doesn't take me seriously and continues with said games.

"Who are you texting?" Evan questions sharply, watching me from the threshold of the room.

I almost drop the phone like I'm trying to hide incriminating evidence. I've done nothing wrong, and I have proof in my hands that I haven't been imagining him. The Faceless Man is the only one that hasn't been treating me like I've lost my mind. But I can't bring myself to show the messages to Evan, be it for fear that this may just be a trick my mind is playing on me and I'm as crazy as everyone says, or that there really is a man that comes into my room at night and touches me.

I'm not convinced either way.

I try to plaster on an innocent smile, then realize that I wouldn't normally smile at such a question. At least the Lili after the accident wouldn't. The Lili before would have joked and asked if he was jealous. This Lili speaks as little as possible outside of Dr. Mallory's office. "Work."

He eyes me suspiciously but just grunts. "I'm going. You're out of bread."

I don't respond, staying glued to my spot long after my wooden floor creaks beneath his departing steps, and my front door clicks shut.

We used to kiss before he left. We used to say exactly when we would see each other next, like we had to know for certain that the sun would rise the following day. He didn't fill my heart completely, but after this past year and a half, I realize what he did fill was my time and the void of meaningless wandering through life.

My attention focuses on the slight tear in the wallpaper, just above the space Evan had occupied, and all thoughts filter out of my mind until there is nothing but white noise.

You're dissociating, Dr. Mallory told me once. *Your mind is going into a state of refuge.*

I should be over mourning what Evan and I once had. I should be done with grieving my old life. But truthfully, I barely remember it anymore. You can't grieve something you lost, when you don't remember ever having it.

My seemingly perfect boyfriend that isn't so perfect now, the dream job and the sister that I no longer have. The latter I will never forget but the former, I barely remember.

My phone's alarm pulls me from my safe space, the place where no one can hurt me and I can't hurt myself. I start moving on autopilot, grabbing my bag and my keys, then drive across town to get to work just as rush hour starts.

I've made a rule not to check my locker as soon as I start because I never know what I might find in there.

The morning goes by in a flurry of orders, and like Evan suggested, I try harder. I plaster a charming smile on my face even though I know it doesn't meet my eyes, and I ask ungrateful customers about their morning. As Evan said, I'm out of bread and he's not working as much, meaning that I can't steal packets of instant noodles and granola bars from his house without him noticing. Unless I asked...

No, I promised myself never to ask him. So I have to earn some money.

It's just a coffee shop. No one tips well when they're just trying to get their dose of caffeine on the way to a job they likely hate after probably needing to wrestle getting their kids into a car and then sit in traffic for the next hour. If I were in their position, I'd be in no mood for small talk and forking out extra cash for the barista that's making me face my terrible life.

The rush dies down, and the tip jar remains as pathetically empty as it was yesterday. A lone glass of water atop the counter summons me closer, left discarded by one of the customers. As I pick it up, I become deaf to my surroundings, suddenly transfixed on the reflection of the water: a dark cloud hidden beneath a hood.

Awareness prickles my skin and I narrow my eyes at the reflection.

A soft breath fans the side of my face before whispering, "*Soon, my night monster.*"

The glass drops from my hand as I spin around, even though I know that I won't find him there. Instead, I swear I see Dahlia standing on the other side of the window outside. But she isn't there either.

My heart thunders against my chest, and everything crashes back to me, bombarding every one of my senses. The black t-shirt sticking to my back, my black jeans digging into the rolls of my stomach and my scars, the smell of coffee, the crying child, the abstract paintings.

Too much. It's all too much. I want to scream at him to leave me alone. Beg him to show me his face. Was losing them not enough of a punishment for living? Now he has to haunt me, hunt me, taunt me. What does he think he'll get? Does he want to break me? Well, I'm already broken. Hurt me? Fine, I know what pain is. But *this?* Whatever twisted game this is, it needs to end. Even if I've sometimes enjoyed it.

I'm not entirely sure the Faceless Man is real but I know for certain that I'm imagining Dahlia. She's dead. She's never coming back. I just need to face her. One day. *Not today,* I tell myself.

I stumble back when soft hands touch my skin, thinking that they're *his*. And for a split second, the one word that crosses my mind at the touch is *finally.*

"Sorry, I didn't mean to startle you. Are you alright, Lili? You're looking a little pale." Brit is younger than me, but she's more put together than I will ever be. Ever the duty manager, she starts cleaning up the mess before I respond, but she glances up at me with her concerned hazel eyes.

I nod, then shake my head. "I'm going for a break, just a dizzy spell."

"Well, you can take the rest of the day off—"

"*No,*" I blurt. I can't afford to miss any work. "I just haven't eaten, that's all."

I try to hide my trembling hands in my apron, and force myself not to look around to see if I can catch him staring at me. Or worse, to imagine Dahlia again.

She frowns, but nods her head. I run to the break room before she can change her mind and let one of the other staff take their break first. My bag is on the table where I left it, and I fumble with the zipper and rummage through its contents until the orange pill bottle is in my grasp. I swallow the medication dry without looking at it first, biting the inside of my cheek to stop myself from choking on the rancid taste.

My head falls forward between my shoulders as I grip the table, trying to get my breathing back when I notice my phone peeking out of my bag. He texted me. That means I can finally respond and let him know exactly what I think of his games.

I waste no time pulling out the phone to tap out a message.

Me: Leave me alone!

Unknown Sender: Never,
my precious flower.

My breath catches once more, then again when I remember that it's time to face my locker. Brit always reprimands me for being the only staff to leave their belongings on the table. Saying that the owner was nice enough to get us lockers, so we should use them, and that a messy break space leads to a messy workspace.

The few steps it takes to get to my locker are filled with foreboding. Maybe a hint of excitement. I never know what lingers behind the pale blue aluminum door. Maybe a gift? Another letter?

He left the first letter on the pillow beside my head.

We meet again, my night monster.

I had just got out of the hospital two weeks prior, and the letter almost sent me right back. I boiled it down to a sick joke, and forgot about it, focused on recovering and grieving; at least tried to do the latter.

I can still hear everyone tell me that it's a miracle that I'm alive, that no one should have survived the crash that was meant to kill me. It almost killed me. I wish it did. I was in a coma for a month, then hospitalized for another month before they sent me home with nothing but pain meds and the trauma to keep me company.

Right before the car wrapped around the tree, I had felt the call: Death. I was ready for it to take me with open arms.

But it didn't want to take me.

It took my sister instead. She and her deadbeat boyfriend who got behind the wheel after insisting that he only had one bottle.

Dahlia's dead, and I'm alive. My other half. My twin.

They didn't mention anything about hallucinations after the accident, even though I told them that there was a man in a hood standing by my bed, that he left a single lily on top of my chest. The doctors waved it off as a side effect of the medication and the shock of losing Dahlia. I told them that it was the Grim Reaper. But they looked at me with a strained expression and told me to just rest.

A phase, they called it.

I brought the lily home, because after a month it hadn't withered away. The nurse said that it must be just like me; a survivor defying all odds. The lily now sits in the darkness of the drawer, surviving again and again and again, just like me. Waiting for a death that never comes. Solace that never happens.

Cockroach, I heard one of Evan's friends call me after yet another failed attempt at seeing the Grim Reaper. But I've stopped attempting. I don't like failing.

I thought it was just the medication from the hospital that played tricks on my mind. Then I was convinced that it was just an impractical joke. Then I opened my locker at work to find a new lily inside. It withered away days later only to be replaced by another in the locker with a note that read:

You will be mine.

I got mad at Evan, accusing him of playing such a disgusting joke. He denied it, so did everyone else. But still, the letters kept coming, appearing in more places they shouldn't: in my coat pocket, my car, my handbag. They haven't stopped since, incessant in nature.

Biting the bullet, I twist the locker door and mentally prepare myself for whatever he might have left me today.

Last time it was a rose quartz skull, the time before that it was caviar—I told Brit that I'd never tried it. Before that, a wad of cash—the most practical gift that he has ever left me. But he always leaves me with at least one lily, whether it's at home or at work. Always a single white lily.

I open the door and a tremor runs down my spine as I reach for the brown parchment and unroll the thick paper, the feeling of being watched prickling my neck.

Not even a sunrise compares to your beauty.

Heat tints my cheek, but I force myself to stamp it down. The only times the word 'beautiful' has been used to describe me since the accident was in a newspaper article that called me a "beautiful tragedy" and these notes from the Faceless Man. I never thought that I would want validation from a man who is a complete mystery, but I've become obsessed with it.

It's more than an obsession. It's a craving. A need.

As much as I want him to get out of my life, he's the only reason that I haven't felt completely alone since Dahlia died. A part of me never wants it to end in fear that once he leaves, I'll realize that he's taken the lifeboats from a sinking ship.

Does that make me as crazy as they claim? Or does it just make me human?

The house sits empty when I arrive home. Just as it always is.

My shift finished without any hiccups, but my feet ache and my stomach hasn't stopped groaning from not having eaten anything in twenty-four hours.

I throw a pizza in the microwave and eat in silence, staring at the charcoal smear above the stove.

The lack of sleep from last night is getting to me. My body drags me down as I go about my night routine and stand in front of my prescription drawer. The medications to stop the hallucinations and the anxiety are enough to put me to sleep. Staying asleep is another matter entirely.

When I dream, I know that I dream of *him*. I don't remember what happens in the dream, so I can't know for sure. But I'm certain that it's him. The only dreams that I remember are of the night of the accident.

I couldn't hear his black boots crunch the leaves as he walked toward me, Dahlia's car blazing behind him with her in it. I couldn't hear any of it. The doctors told me that I flew out of the window upon collision, landing in the dirt with glass sticking out of my body and my neck turned to the side. The faulty seatbelt was the only thing that had stopped me from burning alive.

I couldn't move to look at him as he kneeled next to me and trailed a finger down my bloody cheek and whispered, *"Not yet, my Lilith."*

Dr. Mallory's pills track down my throat and I drag my feet to my room. I check that the nanny cam has enough battery and the windows are locked before falling into bed and letting the medication-induced sleep take me under.

"So sweet. So beautiful. My precious little flower." His voice comes from behind me.

I gasp and spin around. For once, he's there. In a cloak standing in the middle of a beach before a storm. The waves roar as they crash against the shore, deep blue beneath the slate gray sky.

The wind wraps around my bare arms, whipping the white dress around my legs. But I don't feel cold. I don't feel nature's bite at all. When I look down, I finally notice his symbol drawn in the sand, with me standing at the edge of it.

At once, the sounds disappear even though the waves become ravenous and lightning splits the sky. The distance between us closes until he's a matter of steps away.

This is a dream, but it feels so real at the same time. Have I been here before? Why does this place look so familiar?

The Faceless Man reaches out and trails a pale finger down my cheek just as he did the night of the accident. The touch is so warm and tender, and I want so badly to tear that hood from off his head to see what he looks like. I want to see *all* of him. I've already seen the way his clothes strain to contain the muscles hidden beneath the dark layers. I deserve so much more.

His fingers move down to the back of my neck and he pulls me closer to him. Still, I cannot see what is hidden beneath the shadows of his hood. I should pull away from him, tell him to go to hell for hunting me like I'm prey.

"You are a vision of pure beauty, Lilith."

No one calls me that; both Lilith and 'pure beauty'. The shock of the words doesn't stop the shiver from running down my spine. I like my name on his lips—if he even has them.

"What's your name?" I say.

His other hand comes up to trace the curve of my lips. "What would you like to call me?"

"You're the Faceless Man."

His laugh rumbles like the sea, and I almost inch closer just to drink in more of the sound. Maybe even lay my head against his chest to feel its vibrations. "Only because your eyes are closed, my love."

My toes curl into the black sand. I tell myself it's because I miss the sensation of having sand between my toes. Not because hearing him say 'my love' in something other than a whisper has sent molten heat through every corner of my being.

I stare at his hooded form and look around the expanse of sea and sand. "What do you want from me?"

"Everything."

I swallow. I have nothing to give. No money, no happiness, no faith. I'm an empty woman with a heart that never truly beats. I may have a home, but I don't truly belong there.

The hand holding the back of my neck moves, tangling his fingers within my hair as his thumb continues to skate along my lips and down the column of my throat.

"Why?" I finally say.

"Because you were made for me, Lilith. My perfect other. Fate has aligned and brought you to me."

I try pushing against his chest, only because I know that's what I should be doing. Beneath my hands are nothing but fabric and his corded muscle, requiring no further effort than existence to fight against my fruitless attempts.

"You aren't real." None of this is real. This is all just a bad dream. Any second I will wake up to the sound of the alarm and this will all be over. I'll be back to only knowing the sound of his voice through ominous whispers and the fantasies that play out in my head when I read his more *sinful* letters.

His hooded head moves down until the soft material is pressed against my face. "You cannot run from me, because I will catch you. You cannot hide from me, because I will find you. I have smelt your scent, let it linger on my skin, you are imprinted in my memory. You are mine, Lilith. There is nothing you can do to escape me."

I shake my head as he pulls back and flushes my body against his, all hardened and warm like a summer's day, yet cold like winter's first frost. Each syllable from his lips is a rope winding tighter and tighter around me, holding me in place. I don't want to leave. This feels like the one thing I have wanted most: peace.

"Who are you?" I whimper, wanting to feel more than just his muscles beneath the cloak. I want to travel the length of his jaw to feel if he has stubble or a beard. I want to know if gray eyes will stare back at me, or maybe brown or blue?

I shouldn't feel like this, I shouldn't be doing this, not when Evan is asleep on the other side of town. Who is this hooded man? The man that came to me at the accident, who stood next to my bed in the hospital when I should have been taking my last breath, who sends me letters and brings me gifts, even when I am at my lowest.

"I am anyone you want me to be." His hand slithers down from my hair, to the valley of my spine, and settles at the soft curve of my waist. The move feels so natural, like he has done this a thousand times and we are just lovers reuniting once more. "I shall give you a hint: Just as a ship comes to harbor, our meeting is inevitable, my darling Lilith. At the corner of the earth, I will wait for the ship to come. Maybe not today, maybe not tomorrow, but I will be there to greet you and all the souls that will come after."

The Faceless Man. The Nameless Man. "Why can't you just tell me your name?"

He cocks his head to the side as if studying me. But I don't feel his scrutinizing gaze, only one of sweet adoration that sends pools of lava to my core. He pulls me even closer, just when I thought it wasn't possible.

"You know my name, my night monster." He cups my face in his hand and lowers his head to mine, but all I see beneath the hood is darkness.

"Why do you keep calling me that? Do you think I'm a monster or something?" I don't mean to sound as needy as I do, but the thought that I lived at Dahlia's expense is killing me inside.

"Oh Lilith, my sweet, sweet flower." I can't see it, but I know that he's smiling down at me. "Lilith, Adam's first wife, was banished from the garden of evil for disobeying the orders of men. Ask who Lilith is, and you will receive a different answer: A she-demon, a spirit that brings death, a creature of the night, the deadly sin of lust, a night monster. But if you ask me of my Lilith? I will tell you that she is *everything*. Every gust of wind, every fallen leaf, each drop of rain."

"But why?" I squeak, probably looking as pathetic as I sound. I want so much from a man I don't even know.

Tingles cascade over my skin with his soft chuckle. "You have asked many questions, my dear lily. It is my turn to ask just one."

My breath catches with anticipation as my body melts into his wandering touch. His finger runs over my lips once more and stops.

"Tell me, do you taste as good as you look?"

My eyes widen as his finger parts my lips, and I open my mouth on instinct, tasting the sea on his skin. Without another thought, I close my lips around him, tongue caressing his finger, and he shudders beneath my hands as a low growl builds in his chest.

He pulls his finger out and I'm shocked at the feeling of loss that strikes through my heart. Fingers disappear into the shadows of his hood, tasting me just as he said he would.

"Fucking intoxicating," he rasps.

Unsure what to say, I stare at my fingers pressed against his chest and mutter, "Thank you."

He makes a sound of approval. "Oh, my precious flower. The fates have truly made perfection." He tips my chin up to look at him. "I cherish our time together. Soon, a lifetime will become an eternity. But for now, it is time for you to wake up." He swallows my gasp when soft lips press against my own. "I will see you again, little love."

CHAPTER THREE

LILITH

MY LIPS STILL TINGLE from the feel of his, my waist still burns from his commanding touch. But it was just in my head.

I'm not crazy. It was just a vivid dream.

A *very* vivid dream. One that I coincidentally remembered for once.

I kept saying that to myself, over and over this morning, staring at the reflection in the mirror, and once again mourning the Lili that died that day. I can't talk to Dr. Mallory about all the things the Faceless Man said to me, the way it made me want to squeeze my thighs together with the thought that he'll be left with the taste of me lingering on his skin. But it was a dream; I just wish it wasn't.

All Dr. Mallory would do is change my medication or up the dosage, but I can't afford to see her again. Going to her three weeks in a row is not something my bank account is equipped for.

I can't even afford to replace the microwaved pizza from last night. I just have to hope that Brit, in her good graces, might let me take home any leftovers though there usually aren't any on a weekend. If I take the medication as soon as I get home, I'll be too sleepy to be hungry. That is the cheapest idea.

The drive to Evan's place feels longer than usual, my mind reeling too much to hide in the recesses of my 'safe space'.

I start a little later on Saturdays and last night Evan texted to complain about his bad headache, meaning that he won't be able to do our Saturday breakfast—not that either of us has anything more than toast to offer the other. It's not like we have had breakfast on Saturdays often anymore.

Evan lives in a house in the student area of town. It's within walking distance of campus, even though his job involves building houses with his hands and not paying someone else to read a book.

The weatherboards of the house could use some cleaning, but otherwise the place is as you would expect from student housing. A couple of empty beer bottles are piled on the porch, a makeshift flower pot made from broken tires along the driveway, and the floral netting in the kitchen has a tear in it that is visible from the street.

One of the flatmates, Madeline, usually makes sure that Evan and Tom keep the flat nice and reasonably tidy, so at least it doesn't feel like I have to wipe my feet just to go outside.

I help myself into the property, trying to keep my movements as silent as possible. Madeline works dinner and bar shifts at a nearby restaurant, while Tom does security at night over at the university. Usually, I won't see them come out of their rooms until the after-noon.

Madeline's boyfriend, Nate, is pouring himself coffee as I walk in. The pitiful look he gives me makes my skin crawl and still I force myself to smile at him, but he looks away like the sight of me hurts him.

I follow the sound of hushed murmurings to the back of the house, where I find Evan and his strands of golden hair that shimmer in the sun and the smell of weed heavy in the air. Evan never used to smoke, but the accident was hard on him too. Dahlia's boyfriend was one of his closest friends.

Sitting next to Evan on a portable lawn chair is a girl around my age, with hair spun from pure obsidian and skin of dazzling sepia. She looks up at me with the most enchanting brown eyes and quickly turns away. When I look at Evan, he only frowns as if I've interrupted something important.

She wraps her baby blue cardigan tighter around herself and stares at the unkempt lawn, avoiding eye contact with me.

I've never met her before. Logic and reason tell me that she's probably Tom's girlfriend of the week. But reality tells me that Tom's girlfriends don't stick around long enough to share a joint with Evan on a Saturday morning.

After my dream of the Faceless Man, I thought I'd draw my eyebrows on and apply a black line along my lids so that maybe I might feel as beautiful as the man in my dreams thinks I am. But even with the obsidian-haired girl's flimsy pajama shorts and her well-worn woolen cardigan, I feel so inferior. How could the Faceless Man leave letters claiming that I'm beautiful when people like her exist? I wonder what it's like to wake up and know what being pretty feels like.

"What are you doing here?" Evan says, lowering the joint to the ashtray. Heavy bags beneath his eyes that tell a story of a sleepless night.

I pull my bag off my shoulder and start rummaging through it. "You said that you had a really bad headache." I manage to find the painkillers that I dropped in there last night—before the dream—and hold out the packet to him. "So I brought you some medication."

Evan looks at my outstretched hand, then back at me. He blinks like I've said something crazy, then something in his eyes shifts, and he softens. "Thanks. The headache is gone now. But I thought I told you not to come by today."

The small cardboard box bends in my grip when I drop my hand to my side and swing my attention to the obsidian-haired girl and her blue cardigan like she has something to add. Still, she doesn't look up at me.

"You told me that you were sick, so I thought I'd do something nice and—"

He yanks the box of painkillers out of my hand and huffs. "Thank you for your help, but I never asked for it."

I grit my teeth. The girl gets up and goes back into the house without looking at either of us.

"Shouldn't you be at work already?" he pushes, barely avoiding watching the girl walk away.

"Who is she?" I blurt. *Just say those five words, Lili.*

Evan hangs his head back on the deckchair and groans. "Don't be like that. I didn't ask for a jealous girlfriend. Just chill the fuck out, alright?"

Heat stings the back of my eyes, and we both tense when three ominous knocks sound from under the house. It sounds exactly as it did yesterday morning in my apartment. Evan rises to his feet, assessing the lawn, the unease clear in his wrinkling forehead. He turns back to look at me and his gaze drops to my chest.

"When did you get that?"

I follow his stare to the center of my chest where a silver pendant hangs from a chain: A triangle within a circle. The symbol that the Faceless Man marks my skin with. The same symbol I was standing on at the beach in my dream.

Blood rushes through my ears and I squeeze the pendant in my palm, not sure if I am trying to hide it or trying to pretend that last night's dream didn't happen, and that I never tasted his skin.

The urge to tell Evan that this is the symbol that I was telling him about for the past year dies before it makes it to my tongue. He won't believe me, he'll just keep thinking that I'm completely insane.

When I look back up, I almost stumble back. The Faceless Man stands directly behind Evan, towering over him and shrouding him with shadows. With a blink, the Faceless Man is gone.

"Oh, uh, I just found it in my closet."

Evan looks at me like he doesn't believe me, but doesn't push further. "As long as you didn't waste money on it."

I nod as the edges of my vision blur. The Faceless Man wasn't behind Evan. The Faceless Man wasn't here. He doesn't follow me to Evan's. He *never* follows me to Evan's. I need to leave. I can't keep standing here while Evan looks at me like I *am* crazy.

"I need to go to work," I mumble under my breath and all but run back to the safety of my car to swallow the familiar white pill without water.

It's just a hallucination. Just like when you see Dahlia. The Faceless Man did not follow you here. You're just worked up from the dream.

I count to ten and open my eyes, instantly wishing that I didn't, because the words that I just told myself make me a liar. The tears threaten to fall, but I don't let them, not when I can see Nate standing in the kitchen, heating the side of my face with his pity-filled stare and a brown parchment on top of my console holding my gaze:

> *When death comes knocking, it will not wait for you to answer the door.*

It's midday by the time I have my break. The Saturday and Sunday rush are always the worst, but at least the tip jar doesn't look as measly.

Like clockwork, I stand in front of my locker, wondering what might greet me. The Faceless Man already left one letter today, maybe he won't leave another after what he said when I saw Evan yesterday? I know that the thought is just a delusion, because there's no telling when he contacts me, especially now that he apparently has a phone.

As expected, a single lily greets me when I open the door. Evan told me to stop buying them because he's sick of seeing them. I don't even like flowers, let alone lilies. He should know I'm not the one buying them.

The resemblance to my name isn't lost on me, it was an amusing gift at first. Now it feels like there's something that I'm not getting.

Next to the lily is another rolled-up brown parchment. This time, before I unroll the note, I bring it closer and inhale deeply. It smells like a forest in the morning when dew still dots the leaves and the mist still swirls around your legs. But it also smells like the ocean breeze at night, freeing, yet cloying, from the unknown that lies within the darkness.

I unroll the paper and fresh tears gather but don't fall as I read the note:

> *You will bloom, my sad flower. You already have the*
> *earth; I will bring you the sun.*

I tuck the note close to my chest and lean my head against the aluminum locker and fist the necklace he gave me. The Faceless Man is the only one who sees me. Like I don't need to utter a word and he'll know everything there is to know about me. Sometimes I think that he might know me better than I know myself, but then I remember, I may just be as crazy as they say.

My shift ends in a whirlwind of trouble: spills, broken glasses, angry customers, threats of a lawsuit, and to top it off, someone stole all of the money out of the tip jar. Meaning that tonight's gourmet meal will come in the form of antipsychotics made by Johnson and Johnson. But already my stomach aches for something *substantial* to eat, not just a kids' sized packet of chips that one of my coworkers gave me and the chicken sandwich that I'm guessing the Faceless Man left in my locker, but I couldn't stomach.

I almost have to stop and rest as I walk up the stairs to my apartment. Exhaustion weighs on my shoulders and my lower back hurts from being on my feet all day. A bath would be great, but we can't always get what we want. Not when electricity is so expensive, and my patience would be far too thin to wait for the tub to fill.

When I finally make it to my floor, I have to angle the key just right to unlock it. I step into my place, blissfully ignorant with nothing but food and sleep on my mind. As soon as the smell of lasagna drifts through the air and makes my mouth water, I mutter, "God, I really am going insane."

Nothing screams *crazy* like smelling your favorite food when you're delirious with hunger.

I flick the light on and blink. I blink again, thinking the sight in front of me will change and my delirious mind will snap out of it. But it stays exactly the same.

On my kitchen island is a single candle, its flame flickering in time with my pounding heart. Beneath it, a perfectly white plate and silverware that probably costs more than every item I own in the kitchen. Then the sight that truly has me breathless: perfectly cooked lasagna, a plate of sliced ciabatta with garlic butter and melted cheese, and a bottle of wine.

My three favorite things.

For the first time in a while, a real smile tugs at my lips. Without thinking I reach into my bag to fish out my phone to dial the number at the very top: Evan.

I start hobbling toward the bedroom while stripping out of my clothes that smell like stale milk and a crappy day.

He picks up on the third ring. "Hello?"

"Thank you," I say breathlessly. "I love it."

I don't know how he managed to pull this off with finances being so tight, but this is the sweetest thing he's done for me since the accident. He must have felt bad for manhandling me the day before and being a dick yesterday morning.

"Uh, okay?"

I tie the cheap silk robe—that's oddly softer than usual—tightly around my waist and pull on some underwear. For one blissful moment, I feel like the old Lili who walked around the house with a robe and a glass of wine while music played in the background. But the thought dies when I hear feminine giggles on the other side of the phone, followed by Evan harshly whispering, "Shut up."

The worst part is that it doesn't sound like his flatmate's laugh.

Logic tears at the joy I felt and steals the smile that was on my lips only seconds ago. Reality is the worst pain there is. Would he not join me if he went through the effort of making all of this? Wouldn't he wait at the apartment to see my reaction? How did he even get inside without a key? Where did he get the plates and the silverware? Since when does he even cook?

The creak of the wood beneath my feet is louder than ever before, but I'm deaf to the words coming out of Evan's mouth about how busy he will be and how he won't be able to see me. Then I stop in front of the counter and properly take in the setup, including the brown parchment sitting on the bench, just above the plate. With hesitant hands, I unroll the letter:

A feast worthy of my creature of the night. Enjoy your meal, my love.

I press the big red button on my phone, hanging up the call even though words keep coming out of Evan's mouth.

The Faceless Man did all of this. How did he know that it's my favorite food when I haven't had it since before the accident?

I could call the police and tell them that someone did all of this, and that this whole time I was right. But they wouldn't believe me anyway. Part of me wants to knock on my neighbor's door and give them all of the food just so the Faceless Man doesn't think that he has me wrapped around his finger.

That would be a waste of food; he does. He well and truly has me hooked. It terrifies me and thrills me all at the same time.

It's just one meal, I try to rationalize with myself. *It's not like you have anything else to eat. Plus there's enough there to freeze for the next few days. But what if he starts doing this every night?*

My stomach decides for me, and I'm pulled to the seat and pile my plate. Actually, I wouldn't mind coming home to this every night: a candlelit dinner with food that smells like it was made by the gods.

I hesitate when I reach for the wine bottle. I have barely eaten today, and I'm pretty sure my medication came with a big warning not to consume alcohol. I've followed that rule since the day I started it, but the medication clearly isn't working...

What's the worst that could happen if I drink? I start hallucinating, I go crazy? It can't possibly be worse than the cards I've already been dealt.

When a faceless man brings you the best meal you've ever eaten and a bottle of wine that has the logo embossed into the glass, wouldn't it be rude not to try everything that he has to offer?

The red liquid sloshes into the brand new wine glass, and the aroma of it scratches the memories of the old Lili. I was never a connoisseur of wine but even I know that this is *good* wine. I down the glass before I think better of it and pour another one, taking big sips between every mouthful of food.

With each passing second, my body feels lighter and lighter and my numb thoughts defrost. But my free mind doesn't cause any pain, only a hollow giddiness that makes me grab my phone to play music.

The melody fills the void of silence, though the lack of company sings louder. I need more than just letters or random texts. I crave conversation and physical touch. I can't even remember the last time Evan and I were intimate. It must have been at least four months ago, and there was nothing memorable about it.

When I've eaten more than I have in weeks and the wine has done superior work at making me feel *better* than any of Dr. Mallory's drugs, I reach for my phone and go into the message thread with the '*unknown sender*'.

My fingers start moving across the keyboard, only for my drunken mind to think of something better. Brazen and completely idiotic, I rush into my bedroom and tear out a page from my notebook and scrawl:

Join me next time.

Instead of rolling the paper, I fold it into what has to be one of the worst paper planes I have ever made and leave it exactly where he left my letter.

I place the fancy new cutlery in the kitchen sink and run water over it, not trusting myself to wash it in this state.

I check that the paper plane is exactly where he left his note, and lock myself in the bathroom. The floor spins beneath me and I'm not quite sure how I feel about leaving a message for him. I'm basically inviting him to keep haunting me. It was a stupid idea, ridiculous, really.

I don't wait for the water to warm before stepping under the showerhead. I want it to wash away my thoughts and all the scars on my body that the accident left behind.

He clearly has no intention of actually speaking to me. If he hasn't done so in a year, it makes very little sense that he will start now. But he's becoming so much more forward now, testing the boundaries that I thought he put in place.

Dread becomes a second heartbeat in my chest. What if he sees it and doesn't respond? But what if he sees it and *does* join me? I don't know which one would be worse: meeting my stalker, getting rejected by him, or becoming penpals with him?

I don't know how long I stand there, swaying from foot to foot, while my thoughts play in a loop. Eventually the water turns cold again and I rush out before it can chill me to the bone.

The threadbare towel barely holds when I wrap it around my body. It strains against my breasts and I have to clutch the fabric just in case I flash someone from the apartments across the street.

A swirl of emotions clogs my throat when I find that my paper plane has been replaced with another brown parchment. I brace myself for the rejection, to be told that it was the worst idea he's ever heard. Instead, heat burns my skin and the air around me becomes too much to handle.

You are the only thing that I will be tasting.

When I think of the other night's dream, it isn't his fingers I'm imagining in my mouth, but his cock. I'd taste him and imprint it into memory. I'll look up and see nothing but darkness beneath his hood, the storm becoming angrier with each rumble of his chest. He'll pound into me, tearing me from the inside out, and every moment will feel like ecstasy. Lightning will light up the sky as he releases himself into my mouth.

I shift my hips and try to dispel the imagery and feelings as wetness pools between my legs. I tear another page out of my notebook and scribble:

Then let me see you.

I fold the note into an origami crane and place it where his letter sat, then pack away the leftovers while nursing another glass of wine. There's enough left for me not to worry about food for the next couple of days. *Thank you, Faceless Man.*

When the bench is completely cleared and the candle snuffed out, I pad drowsily over to my bedroom, slip into my robe, then crawl beneath the sheets.

Just before sleep takes me, I realize three things: I didn't take my medication, I'm still wearing his necklace, and my paper crane wasn't on the bench when I went to bed.

CHAPTER FOUR

LILITH

DARKNESS SWIRLS ABOVE, a pool of ink and charcoal. I swear I can see faces in the shadows, ascending into the beyond.

I've heard that black holes are stars that have collapsed in on themselves and when they do, shockwaves ripple into space, never to be complete again. From then on, a once shining star becomes a waste of space, living dead, pulling gravity so that not even light can escape.

My fingers twitch, wanting to reach for it, wanting to be pulled into the bowels of obsidian so that maybe when I close my eyes, I finally won't open them again.

Light reaches for the edges of the darkness, like murky waters clawing at the sand. The orange light of a hundred candles flickers and dances across the trees, casting skeletal shadows from the leaves. It smells like an extension of the Faceless Man, the sinister side that will only come out at night. Despite the ominous place, I feel like I've seen it somewhere before.

My heart skips a beat when I actually *feel* my surroundings. Instead of a damp forest floor, I'm splayed across a bed of the softest velvet. The chill of the air doesn't bite my skin. Insects hum all around, and at once, the orchestra stops.

"You look beautiful in your bed. But you are utterly breathtaking in mine."

I gasp as I jolt upright to see him leaning against a tree, and I'm winded by the sight of him. His face is still concealed beneath his hood, but his sleeveless cloak parts to reveal a gallery of moving tattoos along his skin, and pants that hang dangerously low on his hips. Everything about him is deadly, and pure sin. Each shadow cast across each muscle on his stomach is another nail in my coffin, pushing me deeper and deeper into the bed.

I track each swirling tattoo across his chest and down his arms. In the flickering candlelight, shadows dance along his forearms and hands, making each protruding vein seem intimidating and mouth-watering. I wonder what those hands would look like wrapped around my neck. Would his tattoos mock me as he takes me to within an inch of my life, squeezing tighter and tighter while light dances behind my vision?

I suck my bottom lip as I follow the line going down his stomach, then the deep V leading to a place that I have only ever seen in my imagination. Though, I guess a dream constitutes my imagination. But I swear the bulge of his pants moves when I lock my sight on the large dent.

I look down at myself and immediately become self-conscious. I'm in nothing but his necklace and a thin white linen robe that splits just below the area that should be kept hidden, and the top dips low to my navel, a hint of my scar peaking through. I scramble to right the gown, but it does nothing to hide my nipples that can be seen through the fabric.

The fact that I can't tell where he's looking only makes me more self-conscious, like maybe he doesn't like what he sees, or maybe he's about to go in for the kill.

"Why are you here? What is this place? Where am I?" I pester him with questions, hoping he'll answer.

I take the time to properly look around. The bed that I'm on is in the middle of a clearing, surrounded by a hundred candles of varying sizes, forming the shape of the Faceless Man's symbol. Only this time, I'm in the middle of it.

It's like I'm being offered up to a higher power, a sacrificial lamb here for the slaughter. Would I say no, or would I let him have his way with me?

It doesn't really matter what I do, I realize, because *this is just a dream.* I'll wake up tomorrow feeling even more guilty and no less lonely. I'll be back to having contact and connection through the form of one-sided letters. Well, assuming he responds to me.

I run my fingers through the soft red velvet blankets and matching cushions. Grabbing the blanket, I try to pull it up to cover myself so he doesn't see how hard I'm squeezing my legs together or just how obvious my nipples are at the sight of him like that or any trace of my scars.

Just beyond the line of candles, the Faceless Man says, "When my dark storm summons me with the promise of letting me taste her, I come."

The space between my legs grows damp, and it only gets worse when he pushes off the tree and stalks toward me. A predator that has finally cornered his prey. A demon that has finally found a soul.

When he steps over the candles, they blaze even brighter. Goose-bumps pebble along my skin, but not from the cold.

Even though I can't see his face, he's walking toward me like he's going to devour me, lick and bite every inch and not leave a single crumb.

"I didn't summon you," I whisper, foolishly crawling as far back from him as possible.

He stops and cocks his head. "No?"

I blink, momentarily transfixed at the sight of his body from his nearness. I shake my head. "I never did that." I have to tear my eyes away from the hard muscles of his body and to the forestry around. There's almost an otherworldly hue to it. "Is this a dream?"

"No."

He's lying. This must be a dream.

He starts walking again, his steps slower than before like he wants to drag out his hunt until he reaches the end of the bed. I pull my knees to my chest and cross my ankles to hide myself from him.

The bed dips when he leans forward, placing his weight on his hands pressed flat on either side of the bed. Every inch of him is hypnotic, not just because of the smoke dancing on his skin, but because he's sculpted like a Greek god.

"I told you that I will be tasting you." I scream when he darts his hand out to grab my ankle and pull me to the edge of the bed, so that I'm at his mercy. "And I am not a liar, Lilith."

I squirm beneath him when the cold air caresses my center, and I try to shift my hips to tug the robe down, but he grabs my wrists and holds them above my head with a single hand. The combination of the two moves has a whimper escaping my throat. I swear somehow the shadows beneath his hood darken.

"This is just a dream," I say to myself, rather than him.

"Tell me, my love." He drags his free hand from my ankle, up my thigh and to my hip, slowly, ever so slowly, holding it down when I try to shift away from him. Then he moves his hand between my legs. I buckle when a whisper of a touch slithers over my lips, making me feel like this is definitely real.

"Do you often dream of me between your legs?"

As if his soul is pulling away from his body, a dark shadow forms behind him, growing in size and unfurling like a true creature of the night. The shadow has to be eight feet tall at least. It mimics the Faceless Man's every move like it's an extension of himself. Even though I can barely see the shadow's silhouette, I can just make out the barrel chest and the width of his arms that are bigger than the size of my head. Still, this form is identical to the Faceless Man's.

I try to move away as the shadow develops a mind of its own, reaching for my throat and wrapping its cool fingers around it. The pressure doesn't hurt, but it starts a deep pulse between my legs as it—he—steals my breath.

"Are you a monster?" I manage to gasp.

He grazes my glistening heat as a low growl starts in his throat. Then he drags his hand beneath the robe over the soft skin of my stomach to grab a full breast. "He and I are one. Do you think that I am a monster, Lilith?"

I'm too breathless to respond, not for the lack of air, but for the way he assaults my nipple. Twisting and pinching ruthlessly as if it is my punishment for asking such a question.

A shadowed hand reaches down and yanks my robe open, baring me to the Faceless Man and his shadow. I huff out a gargled cry when a shadowed hand slaps my breast, leaving behind a sinful burn. There's no way that he can't see my scars or the way they make me feel like I am *less*. But the way that he's grasping me tells me that he couldn't care less about them. Like he said, he thinks I'm beautiful.

"Answer me. Let me hear your voice."

I whimper and buck my hips up, trying to gain some friction. I feel so pathetic, having a dirty dream about a man I've never truly met. I moan, not recognizing this desperate person that I am, wanting his skin on mine and to be full of everything he wants me to feel.

It has been so long since I've been touched. But ever since that first letter, I've never lacked the feeling of being wanted. The Faceless Man has made sure that the feeling is constant. Still, I have doubts. I need his touch, too.

"No," I choke out. *I think you're an angel,* I want to say. *Saving me from death. Saving me from myself.*

"Do not move your hands from this spot, or you will learn just how monstrous I can be. Do you understand?" The pressure around my throat increases and his hands move to the next nipple, abusing it as he did the other. "Nod your head if you understand."

I nod.

He leans down, blinding me with the darkness beneath his hood. My back arches involuntarily when his chest caresses my nipples.

He pulls my bottom lip between his teeth sharply and my breath stutters. He licks the wound and pulls away, letting go of my throat.

"Good girl."

This is just a vivid dream. This is just a vivid dream. This is just a vivid dream.

The shadowed hands find purchase with my breast, giving them more attention than they've ever received in their life.

"What are you doing?" I pant when he lowers himself until my heat is in the same line of sight as his eyes.

"I brought you a meal. It's only fair that you offer me one in return." He draws a single finger over my clit, then pushes into my entrance and hisses. "So beautiful." I cry out from the combined stimulation of the shadowed hands and his real one. "I can smell your need for me, Lilith. I have made a decision, do you want to know what it is?"

It takes everything in me not to tell him to add another finger and just let me fall off the edge of bliss. The one digit keeps moving in and out of me, curling slightly to hit the spot that will make me see stars. But his lazy motions tell me he's not even trying.

He's playing with his food.

Delirious with need, I forget that he asked me something until a shadowed hand slaps my breast. "Your words, love."

My brain is in too much of a frenzy to think of what it might be. "Yes."

"I'm not just going to taste you. I'm going to hear you scream."

My cheeks burn. "What—"

I swallow my words when another finger is shoved inside of me, and everything around me stops existing. There is only him and the swirls moving across his chest. I don't get a chance to compose myself before he drops his head and starts lapping at my clit like a starved man who has just received his first meal.

"Fuck," he snarls, and it's almost like he's laughing to himself in disbelief as a needy moan leaves my lips when he takes me in between his teeth. "I am going to devour you."

I try to squeeze my legs and am met with a sharp assault to the side of my ass before he grabs the flesh like a lifeline, dulling the pain. One of the hands—I'm too lost in the sea of bliss to determine if it's corporeal or shadow—pries my legs apart, pushing them as wide as they can go, letting the Faceless Man have more of me.

His fingers curl, and I do exactly what he said: I scream. I don't even hear his growls of approval as he continues repeating the motion, flicking his tongue faster and faster, like I will run away any second.

I want to go against his command and let my arms down so that I can pull his hood away or reach beneath it and feel exactly what he's hidden from me.

"Wait, stop." My voice is raspy, the words coming out on two heaving sighs.

He freezes. My stalker and his shadow stop touching my body, and I almost tell them to disregard what I said and keep going. But I don't want to have to call him *the Faceless Man*, not when he's eating me like I'm his last meal.

"What's your name? What are you?" I breathe out, my throat beginning to tingle from my screams.

God, Lili, it's a dream. How the hell would he tell you his name?

"I want you to figure out *what* I am." He kisses the inside of my thigh. "But the only word I want you screaming is my name: Letum."

I bite my tongue because moaning his name is going to be a mouthful. What sort of name is that? Roman? What does it even mean? How did my mind conjure such an ancient-sounding name?

"Okay, *Letum.*"

He snarls and dives back to fucking me with his fingers and licking me like he might find religion somewhere inside me. A shadowed hand fists my hair and pulls me up onto my elbows so that I can watch his ruthless movements. Letum's hood angles upwards, as if he's watching me too, and he's waiting for me to come undone.

I gaze up at the shadow, and just make out the faintest outline of eyes boring down on me, as if committing the sight to memory. Is the shadow just his soul? What exactly is it—he? I don't know.

Letum's hand grips my thigh with his free hand hard enough to leave an imprint on my skin that will bruise come morning, and his shadowed one reaches for my face, tracing my lips like he's trying to capture my moans with his touch so that he can write about it in a letter. The move is so intimate, making my heart squeeze.

"Sing for me, my love," he whispers against my skin as he curls his fingers and hits the part of me that I forgot existed.

I scream his name out like a curse, and buck my hips. Unbridled ecstasy rips through every inch of me. He continues with his feast, sucking and licking until there is nothing left for me to give him, my body and mind going limp with the pleasure I have been starved of.

"Oh, my love," he mumbles against the inside of my thigh, grazing his lips along the soft skin before biting down, leaving small marks along my skin. "Oh, my night monster. You are a dream. Nothing could compare to the taste of you."

Heat flushes my cheeks at the compliment. I have never felt so satisfied. For the first time since the accident, the tension in my body subsides and muscles relax, like I can finally breathe and not feel the weight of everything that's gone wrong.

I watch with curiosity as the shadow moves behind me, pulling me upright and digging its cool fingers into my shoulders,working out the knots.

Letum rises to his feet and places his hands on the bed on either side of me, caging me in between him and the shadow. His hips are in between my legs and it would be so easy to give into the fantasy and feel one of the many things that have been hidden from me. I drop my gaze down to his bulge that is straining against his pants like it is begging to be free. I don't need to let it out of its cage to know that the stretch will sting.

"Use your words," he says, noticing my stare. I reach for the hem of his pants, only for my wrists to be caught in his iron grip. "Your words." He takes my chin and lifts it up to darkness beneath the hood. "Your voice is an aphrodisiac, my Lilith. You should use it more often."

I swallow the lump in my throat and wet my bottom lip. The shadow's massage halts for a moment, as if I've done something to bother it. Then it moves closer, pressing against my back as if it were completely solid.

I look down at his chest, then at his bulge, then slowly make my way back up to his concealed face, taking my time to relish every inch of his body. The pulsing between my legs springs back to life with new vigor. "May I?"

A low chuckle resonates through the forest, and he fulfills another one of my fantasies: He makes a necklace out of his hands by wrapping his fingers around my throat, only he doesn't squeeze. The veins in his arms move and pulse under the candle light. I let myself give into temptation and skim the masculine ridges of his forearms, making his hold around my neck tighten.

The shadow shifts its large hands to knead my breast and send more heat to my core. The shadow's hand practically covers my whole chest, making me feel small and—dare I say it—dainty.

"Lilith. My sweet night monster. I told you that I would taste you. I told you that you would be screaming my name." I swear I can hear the grin on his face in his words "I did not say that I would fuck you."

Embarrassment turns my blood cold. I've been a dark cloud since the accident and have done practically nothing to be appealing or even feel sexy. Even the Faceless Man in my dream doesn't want me. Evan doesn't, so why should Letum—if that's even his actual name—find me attractive with all my scars.

He presses his soft lips to mine, and the smell of morning dew and a summer's breeze wafts over me, dissolving my doubts. His warm breath fans the shell of my ear as he says, "I have longed for the taste of you, and now that I have it, I will never know another. When I fuck you, there won't be any candles. It won't be in a dream. When I claim you, it will be on my terms. But it will not be tonight."

I let a whimper escape my lips, after being left high and dry. He can't seriously just leave me a wet and needy mess and deny me the simple pleasure of a second orgasm, especially when my raw nipples are still getting the shadow's undivided attention.

Letum taps his symbol that is hanging around my neck. "You were made to wear me."

"Please," I whisper, grinding my hips into the bed to reach another release.

"Please?"

He's taunting me, I know he is. He wants me to become completely his, just so that I can give him all of me while he gives me nothing in return. But this is just a dream. He's not real. I remind myself.

"Please," I beg, "Letum."

He growls in approval as the shadows' attention to my breasts becomes rougher and more hungry. I'm too distracted by the shadow to notice that Letum moved his hand until he pressed a heavy thumb right on my clit, sending electric fire straight to my core.

"Go on."

He wants me to say it, to voice my needs. That's the opposite of what has always happened between me and the Faceless Man. I don't voice the troubles on my mind to anyone other than Dr. Mallory. Even then, I don't tell her about my issues with getting food into my cupboard or paying for things. Letum has known exactly what

I need without me having to say it. Whether it's to hear that I look beautiful, or just to know that someone recognizes my pain.

"Please, Letum. I want to come again," I beg, voice low and meek.

He does nothing for a moment, then he finally leans in and kisses me. It isn't hungry or demanding, isn't filled with lust or need. The kiss is one of silent understanding and mutual connection, but also like he's proud of me.

Then he pulls away. Before I can blink, I'm thrown onto my hands and knees. Just as before, the shadow stays behind me. Except this time, a thick finger slides through my wet heat, then pushes into me.

I throw my head back and groan, my eyes automatically rolling to the back of my head. The Faceless Man takes the opening as a chance to grip my hair to force me to look up at him.

One of the shadow's fingers is bigger than two of Letum's. I grind my hips, drawing pleasure from the shadow as his finger slams into me. What does it say about me that the thought of being finger fucked by a shadow that has no real features other than a silhouette is the hottest thing I could ever think of? I want it to be Letum's cock that I'm riding, but my god, the fact that the shadow is near invisible is doing more to me than it should.

I'm whimpering and mewling, teetering on the edge of release, when the shadow's pumps slow, though the hold on my hips doesn't falter. "Relax, my love. I'm not done with you yet."

I frown, only to scream when another finger pushes into my pussy, stretching it to the point of agony. Tears of both pain and pleasure pricks my eyes. It's larger than anything I have ever been with.

"Take all of it." The shadow slowly slides his fingers in until he reaches his knuckle. I moan as I try to accommodate the size and just how deeply inside of me he is. He doesn't start moving again until I curl my back to take him even deeper. "That's it. All of it."

A sharp sting of pain makes me hiss, but I'm too caught up in each thrust to do more than just scream and moan. If this is only a dream, how does it feel so real?

Movement just below my line of sight catches my attention. I try to move my head but his grip in my hair stops me from getting far.

"What are you doing?" I gasp, biting my lip as I pant and try to hold back another scream.

Somewhere under the darkness of his hood, I swear I see a sinister smile flash across his seemingly non existent face. "It's only fair that you taste me too."

My eyes widen before my head is pushed straight down onto his cock. My mouth barely fits around him, still he pushes further inside me. He doesn't make it far before I gag, but he doesn't relent, the sound not a deterrent but an encouragement.

"All of it. Just like I told you to." His voice is firm, not revealing if he feels as undone by me as I am by him.

Tears stream down my eyes as I'm filled so completely by two beings I've never seen the faces of. My jaw aches from how wide I have it open. I try to relax my throat and Letum pushes in deeper.

"My sweet flower, look at you. So beautiful on your hands and knees for me. Tell me, is this what you dream of?"

He tugs on my hair to pull out of me completely, and raises me higher so that my upper body is held up by his grip. Tears wet my cheeks, and saliva drips down the side of my mouth. With his thumb, he swipes the drool and pushes it back into my mouth.

"Is it?"

Never in my wildest imagination would I have thought up the shadow. Now, I wouldn't have it any other way.

The answer would be a confident *yes*. Daydreams, at least.

His letter that asked what I would feel like when I finish on him had such a visceral impact on me that I still haven't forgotten about it half a year later. The mystery of the unknown was a kink in itself, not knowing what he looked like or when I might find him. It made my mind think of things that would certainly make Dr. Mallory up my dosage.

The shadow's fingers pull out of me, leaving me empty and incomplete. I whimper and almost reach back to get the shadow to put his fingers back, or else I'd be finishing the job myself.

"I asked you a question," he warns.

"Keep fucking me, please," I beg. When he doesn't answer, I say, "Please. I need it. Fuck my face, fill my pussy. I just need you to *fill* me. *Please.*"

Letum's body visibly softens. "You're so beautiful when you beg." I cry out when a sharp slap hits my ass so hard that white dots appear in my vision. "But that was not my question."

Why does he have to make me admit those things? This is a dream! I should be the one in control. Though, what's the worst that could happen if I admit it? All that will happen is that I will be ravaged by guilt in the morning.

"Yes," I finally say. He waits for me to continue, and I groan. "I've dreamt about what your cock would feel like inside of me. I have dreamt that I'd open my locker during my break, but instead of a letter or a note, you appear out of nowhere. You grab me by the neck and push me over the table, and you don't stop fucking me until my knees give out and my voice goes hoarse with your name."

Both Letum and the shadow snarl at once. They fill me at the same time and start pounding into me before I get the chance to take a breath. I'm stuck, permanently gagging on his cock while the shadow sinks deeper than I knew was possible.

Pleasure bubbles and boils beneath my skin. I try to stop Letum and warn him that I'm about to fall off the edge straight into the deep end and I'll take him down with me, but neither of them stop their relentless thrusts.

When I can't take it anymore, my hands and knees collapse beneath me. I'm writhing and trembling, trying to take my fill of the explosion of bliss caused by the unknown and his shadow, all while they keep me upright with their continued assault.

Letum's roar shakes the trees and rattles my bones as he releases himself into my mouth. I try to take every sweet drop of him and swallow, laving at every inch of him with my tongue.

"You were more amazing than anything I could have imagined, my midnight storm."

He slowly lowers me onto the mattress while I struggle to keep my eyes open. I'm too exhausted to watch the shadow retreat into Letum. Before I can ask him whether the shadow is his soul as I suspect, I close my eyes and the darkness engulfs me.

I groan when the incessant beeping of the alarm ruins the sensation of the forest air on my skin. Without opening my eyes, I keep slapping the bedside table until I find the culprit that tore me from the best dream I've ever had.

I don't look at the time, just push any random button to snooze the alarm. Last night's alcohol must have really gotten to me, because if anyone told me that I've been hit by a truck, I would believe them.

I shift onto my back and whimper from the ache between my legs—the type of ache that only happens from life changing sex.

My skin pebbles from the morning air, making my painful nipples even more tender. One by one, I peel my eyelids open.

What the hell?

No, I wasn't so drunk that I went to bed *naked*. I'm not a nude sleeper and I most definitely do not go around commando.

No, I wasn't so drunk that I would cover my entire bedroom floor in rose petals.

Red creeps up my cheeks when I realize that he would have seen me naked in my bed and seen my scars. Worse, he could have seen me in god knows what state while I was having the raunchiest dream in my life. Was I moaning in my sleep? Oh god, was he watching?

My thumb grazes the velvety smooth petals, confirming that they are in fact real, and neither I nor he had gone to the dollar store to buy fake ones. I reach for my bedside lamp and turn it on to inspect one of the petals closer. It's of the deepest red I've seen, but there's something off about it, with veins-like threads going through the petal.

Blotches of blue amongst porcelain catch my attention and I discard the petal back onto the floor. Four blue bruises mar my thigh. When I turn my leg, I spot a fifth.

My heart slams against my ribcage. I leap out of the bed like a woman possessed and almost slip on the roses as I head straight for the bathroom. I flip the light switch before I make it inside, and stop dead in my tracks in front of my mirror.

Oh god. Oh god. Oh god.

I turn in front of the mirror, then turn again, angling myself this way and that while trying to convince myself that I'm just imagining things.

The area around my nipples are red and raw, but that can easily be explained away with an excuse I'll think of later. I'll even find an excuse for the five small circular bruises on my hips. There is no explaining away the handprint that covers an entire ass cheek and then some though.

The size of the handprint is larger than anything I've seen in real life. The sting that follows when I touch the welt both shoots heat straight between my legs and fear straight to my heart.

I'm not sure if this is the reason I'm not meant to drink alcohol on my medication, but I swear the handprint is as large as the shadow's hand, and I do vividly recall that it slapped my ass in the dream.

But that's all that it was: *a dream.*

Right?

It must have been a dream. I didn't make my way to a forest where I was practically mauled by a Faceless Man with moving tattoos and a gigantic shadow while lying on a velvet altar in what looked like a sacrificial circle. I'm only a few miles away from forestry, but I didn't walk there naked or in a skimpy robe, and I most definitely didn't drive.

I sprint back to the room, aiming straight for my phone to watch the nanny cam. As expected, half the footage of the night is completely sliced away. One second I'm snuggled up in my robe beneath the sheets, and the next, I'm completely naked with roses blanketing the floor. In the blurry footage, I notice a rolled parchment that slips between my pillows as I sleep.

With my heart caught in my throat, I throw the pillows onto the floor in search of the letter. I jump onto the mattress and lie flat on my stomach as I reach behind the bed, blindly patting the wooden floor until I touch familiar parchment.

My blood vibrates as I fish it out of the darkness, and move to the very edge of the bed near the light.

Keep dreaming of me, my dark love. I'll be back for more.

CHAPTER FIVE
LETUM

For eons I have been tasked with one thing: Bring souls to the afterlife.

Day after day, night after night, with a single touch from my hand, a soul will pass peacefully and their body will sleep for all of eternity. I have known no other life other than this morbid repetition and passionless existence. For eons I have watched humans, standing to the side and waiting until they inevitably pass.

Because I am inevitable.

Poets have written sonnets about me; composers have written music. Beautiful as they may be, they never amounted to anything more than a moment lost to time.

Until *her*.

Lilith, my sweet love. She is a dream and a nightmare, merged into one.

I never thought I would find a woman such as her; a woman who can gaze upon death and bring him to his knees. The sight of her, the smell of her, the *taste* of her, she has made death himself come alive.

Even when fear poisons her blood, I could take a bite out of her and eat the softest flesh. My night monster is perfection, an anomaly in a room of normality, a miracle in the face of wonder. There is nowhere she can run where I will not catch her, nowhere she can hide where I will not find her.

Her soul sings to me like a summer's breeze: fresh and decadent. I have not been able to get enough of her since the beyond called for her. The afterlife wanted her in its grasp, but I wanted her in mine.

Lilith has called for me in the night, begging and pleading for me to take her soul as I should have. The fates can attest to the wrongness of keeping a soul in the mortal plane long past its time. It is the only way I can make her mine for eternity; she must yearn for me as I yearn for her.

Not death, but *me*.

I watch her from the corner of the room as she piles the petals together, biting her lip while sporting my marks on her skin. She fists a plastic bag, convinced that she will discard the maroon flora. But she will not throw away something with life until it has decayed into rot. Not because she values life—no, it's because she values *me*.

Lilith has become my favorite activity, there is nothing dull about her; I yearn to watch her, taunt her, feel her soft flesh beneath my hands.

I have watched her since the moment I saw her lying on the ground, broken and bruised, begging for me to take her away. I stood by her as machines surrounded her when she lay defeated in a hospital bed. She was calling for me every second. They all thought it was the machines keeping her alive, but it was *I* that kept her from death.

Despite the bruises that painted her, the cuts that scarred her skin, and the porcelain hue of her face, she was still the most breathtaking vision I had ever seen in all my eons.

I can still remember the first time that her blue eyes found me at the foot of her bed; it was as if the planets had aligned because finally I have found my one true love. The moment I laid my eyes on her, I knew that she was more than the sun and the stars. She was everything, and I was never going to let her go.

Even at the risk of losing it all, I would fall for her. For if I were Icarus and she were the sun, I would still fly to her with my waxen wings. Her beauty would be worth the pain that I would feel just to reach her.

My dark love does not feel either. She barely flinches when she slices her finger open. She does not smile with her eyes nor does she fear walking alone at night. However, she does feel with me; she feels everything. It is clear when her skin flushes before opening her locker and the way she subconsciously bites her lip before unrolling my letter. Even when she shifts her weight reading one of my more illusive notes. I know she longs for me. My night monster only responds to me.

Seeing her wear *my* mark around her neck pleases me more than I thought it would. The silver symbol glints when it catches the light, making my night monster's eyes sparkle.

Her phone pings from the kitchen, and she sighs, beelining to the device. I follow behind her, enraptured by the movement of her hips beneath her silk robe. It's unfortunate that she has decided to put some undergarments on, but she is no less a sight. The slight limp she has makes up for it, a smile etching its way onto my face.

I curl my fingers into fists as soon as I see his name on her phone. *Evan*. The male who does not deserve her. The only other person that can make her feel, except not in the way she deserves. Every time tears prick her eyes from another one of his comments, is another strike in my ledger.

> **Evan:** Can you transfer money? We're out of green.

We.

Lilith's posture deflates when she reads the message. I left her alone with him because I thought my love would see the leech for what he is: a soul sucker. He lives to tear her down just to use her body to help him up. I gave her the space to pull herself away from him, to use me as her crutch, and throw him aside.

I've proven to her that I'm all she needs. I can give her money, food, attention, and love, for the rest of eternity.

He can give her nothing but disappointment.

She cringes as she opens her bank account, showing the meager nineteen dollars that are meant to carry her for another four days. I caress her arm as she stares at her phone for so long that the screen goes black, but even then she does not move.

It is selfish of me to refuse her soul and force her to continue living. Perhaps it is selfish of me to continue living in the shadows as she goes through her day with reality nowhere in her mind. I can take her pain away, but I won't. Not until she decides to live and she chooses to want me, not for what I can give her, but for who I am.

I leave her for a moment to return to her room while she continues to stare blankly at her phone. Shadows morph and flicker in front of me like a ravenous cloud, until a rolled parchment is floating in the middle of the air.

The hard paper is so insignificant in my hand. It is difficult to believe that something so small has the ability to bring out emotions in her so strong that it shakes her soul, be it rage, joy or even fear.

I lower myself next to the pile that she created and hide the letter beneath a crimson petal. Lilith deserves more than roses or lilies. Would diamonds suffice?

The shadows form once again. A wad of cash appears in the air, held together by a silver money clip with a raven embossed on it.

Her brown bag sits on top of her desk, frayed and peeling, looking as if the handle will snap any second. I hide the money inside with another letter telling her to get something for herself. She never does.

The black bag I made for her is hidden at the back of her closet—the woman's bag that Lilith complimented. As is the winter coat that I made her. Same with the leather boots. Lilith has never knowingly worn anything I've given her—not until the necklace that she still hasn't taken off. She couldn't take it off if she tried, though it appears that she hasn't figured that out yet. There is no clasp, and I have made sure that the thin chain will never break.

However, my little storm has been wearing things that I have made without her even knowing. Replacing the same thing that she has, only better: her jacket now has extra stuffing to keep her warm, the zipper of her jeans no longer catches, and contrary to her belief, she has not gotten over her allergy of cheap metals, for all her jewelry is now made of silver.

Now that she wears my necklace, perhaps she will begin wearing more of my gifts.

What has this *Evan* gotten her in the year and a half I have watched her? Some voucher to a diner that didn't even cover Lilith's meal? Harsh words when she can't provide his fix?

The phone chimes again, and from another room, I can hear her sigh, followed by the sound of her phone clattering on the bench. My sad flower walks back into her room, gaze distant and devoid of emotion—until her mask breaks when she looks at the rose petals. She sucks in her bottom lip as her cheeks turn bright pink.

I smirk, knowing exactly what it is that she's thinking about.

Her head tips to the side as she edges closer to the petals, clearly seeing the latest addition to the pile. I move closer to her and smile, smelling my scent all over her. Does she truly not notice that her robe feels different?

Lilith stands back up and unrolls the letter with hesitant fingers. Her cheeks are no longer a soft pink but a deep red.

She sucks in a sharp breath as she reads it.

Now that I have had a taste of you, I will never let you go. We will be united soon, my storm.

My dark love can tell herself that last night was just a dream. She can fool herself into believing that she has never felt the touch of my lips or the feel of my fingers inside of her. She can even try to forget it.

I never will.

Neither will she, however hard she tries.

She'll convince herself that my note has a different meaning, that I might have done something without her knowing. But she was a very willing participant, and I bet a thousand souls to say that she wants her *dream* to happen again.

I step behind her, letting her feel my presence. I press against the shell of her ear and whisper, "You're mine."

Lilith freezes in her spot like a deer caught in headlights. Her breaths turn erratic as I skim my finger along the outside of her thigh. When I reach the place where my soul's hand marked her skin, her eyelids flutter and her body relaxes into mine ever so slightly.

I follow the curve of her behind until I reach her aching heat. "Are you wet for me, my love?"

A response isn't required, because her entire being shudders when I slip my fingers beneath her underwear. As I thought, she's wet just because of me. Moisture coats my finger as I run it through her seam.

Her excitement was so potent when my soul joined our fun last night. Did she imagine that it was my cock instead of my fingers? Did she wonder what it would feel like to be filled with two cocks at the same time? She will scream in both pain and pleasure, but will her eyes roll to the back of her head? Will her own fingers traverse the planes of her body before finding purchase on her clit and rubbing it until she no longer knows the difference between life and death?

She feels so right in my hands—soaked and trembling. *Fuck*, she has no idea how much she drives me mad, blind with need. I have craved her for so long that to finally have her is the most otherworldly experience.

"Please," she whispers.

Being here with her, skin to skin, soul to soul, is invigorating. Last night we were both split in half, partly here and partly in the place where I wanted to worship her. Not true skin to skin, but soul to soul. We felt each other in the way that mattered.

I run my nose along the column of her neck, breathing in deeply. "Your words."

Her breath catches like it does every time. I slip a finger inside of her and a soft moan leaves her lips that I want to capture and have on repeat forever. Her arms stay locked at her sides while the rest of her melts into me at the smallest touch.

My fingers aren't enough, I need to feel her whole body quake on my cock as I give her all the pleasure that she deserves.

"Words," I warn.

She blinks rapidly as I start picking up my momentum. "What—" she hiccups when I thumb her clit, moving in slow circles that draw bliss and agony all over her features. She's practically riding my hand, and her hypnotic groan makes me add another finger for her to wind herself upon. Her legs shake like she wants to take my fingers deeper as if she needs to be stretched even more than she was last night. "What do you want from me?"

My night monster doesn't wish to deny me. Does she know that she's mine already? Has she submitted to me at last?

The curve of her body is pressed so perfectly against mine. Hell could come between us, and I still wouldn't move.

I massage her heavy breasts as she trembles for more—more of the pleasure that only I can give her. She's so breathtaking. Vulnerable and needy. Dark brown hair tickles my hand as I mark my claim over her swollen flesh. How have I gone a thousand lifetimes without this pleasure? How have I kept my hands away from her for so long?

"My dear Lilith, I told you already. I want everything."

I bite the soft skin of her neck and remove myself from her to hide once more, leaving her hunched over and gasping for breath.

I am a selfish lover. I have given her everything she needs without asking, but I will not give her what she wants unless the words come from her pink lips.

She snaps upright, turning furiously as if I'm not standing right in front of her. The floorboards creak as she storms out into the living area, then the kitchen, as if I might be hiding in the pantry.

Leaving her in a state such as this pains me just as much as it pains her. When her pussy pulsed on my fingers as she came, I knew there was nothing else in this world that could compare.

Lilith belongs to me, wholly and completely. And when the day comes that I claim her, every breath that she takes will belong to me.

She crushes the letter in her hand as she whips open one of the drawers to pull out the orange plastic bottle.

My body tenses as I watch her put one of the pills between her teeth, then flush it down with water.

"Soon," I promise even though she cannot hear me.

Because soon, Lilith will be all mine.

CHAPTER SIX

LILITH

THE MORNING RUSH AT work goes by in a blur. I've been trying to escape my own mind by hiding in it, but my brain hasn't been letting me do it as often as I would have liked. My break eventually comes around, and I find my locker empty except for the shattered pieces of my heart.

It has been five nights since my dream about the Faceless Man. Five days since the last letter that I received from him. Five days since my body has been hung on a string, begging for release that won't come from my own fingers.

How dare he do that to me? He doesn't just get to leave me high and dry like that. He's been toying with me for so long, but bringing me to the brink of an orgasm, and then just leaving me? God, what does that say about me when I haven't been this mad about the stalking or the letters, yet not letting me come is the thing that has me tossing and turning for five nights straight.

I keep wondering if I imagined the whole thing. I mean, he was there one second and gone the next. The nanny cam was wiped of the whole event.

I used to think that he was a ghost. For a solid two months, I dedicated my time, scouring the internet about getting rid of ghosts.

He can get in and out of anywhere without being noticed, disappear into thin air, and it just so happens that only I can see him. I even wore a safety pin at all times because, apparently, it would prick any spirit that tried to touch me. Either his spirit is a masochist or the safety pin was another useless attempt.

I'm not the superstitious type, but I admit, at one point my apartment reeked of garlic before I realized that it was meant to be for vampires. Evan complained about the smell for weeks. After some research I spent my meager funds on sage. The next day the faceless *asshole* left me three bundles of the herb with a note saying, "*Try again.*"

I've crossed off—though not completely—imaginary friends. Because imaginary friends don't leave a grand of cash in my handbag or restock my cupboard with food. I had checked, it wasn't Evan who did it. This leads me to two assumptions: he's a really talented human, or... *No*, that's even less realistic.

Somewhere deep down, I know it wasn't a dream. Not completely, at least. I couldn't sit or walk properly that entire day, and I spent the entire time feeling both thoroughly fucked and not fucked enough.

He said that he has tasted me. How would it be possible for it to be anything other than a dream? How else would he have tasted me like he's claimed? Usually, if Evan so much as turns in his sleep, I wake up. The Faceless Man had been leaving temporary marks on me for a year, never something as permanent as a handprint, bruises, or even a necklace, and I never woke from his ministrations.

But if it weren't a dream and he was with me, why hasn't he reached out to me since that night? I've heard and received absolutely nothing from him. I haven't even seen him in any reflection. He's never left me alone for this long before, and I can't help the pain that has been ballooning in my heart. I've been checking my locker as soon as I get to work. I've even been pulling out my bed every morning to see if a letter dropped behind it. The Faceless Man doesn't want me anymore, maybe he never did. He was just bored and I was easy prey.

Without his letters and little reminders that he exists, I feel the loneliness, ripe and raw. There's a Faceless Man-sized hole in my heart now.

He's left me, and it hurts. He didn't even say goodbye.

All he left behind are patches of violet and green that will eventually fade back into porcelain skin. As if that wasn't enough, he left without saying anything; the last thing he did was leave cash in my purse like I'm some kind of whore.

I bought today's lunch with the Faceless Man's money. Everything I've eaten that was paid with his money has left a sour taste in my mouth and a hollow ache in my chest. Still, I sit at the fold-out table in the break room, on second hand plastic chairs with one of the local school's insignia on it, and I nibble on the food in the hope that it might fill me completely.

I tuck a loose strand of hair behind my ear, brushing the earring I put on this morning to match the necklace. I even put on more makeup than usual so that I might catch his attention or find a letter or even a text that says that he hasn't forgotten about me.

Brit walks into the backroom with an almost innocent look on her face. My brows pull together as she heads straight for me rather than the office.

"Hey, Lili," she starts.

I smile blankly at her, hoping that she reads the room and sees that I want to be left alone. But she has her manager-face on, and that's never a good sign. The last time she looked at me like that, she dropped my hours for two weeks while they were restructuring.

"I didn't want to tell you before because we were swamped." I hold my breath and wait for the inevitable *but*. "We've never had this issue so it must have just slipped your mind. But you're not allowed to wear rings while handling food."

I look at her confused. The words "*I'm not wearing any*" are on the tip of my tongue. I almost let them escape my lips and lie straight to her face. Because when I look down all the evidence is there to prove that Brit is right.

Both happiness and fear strike through me at the sight of the thick gold band wrapped around the ring finger on my right hand. I can just see words engraved into the ring and I have to resist the urge to bring it closer to inspect it while in Brit's presence.

I swallow. I swear it wasn't there this morning. How have I not noticed it?

She watches me curiously, and I try to force a smile. "Sorry. It was an accident."

Brit returns the smile, only hers reach her eyes. "That's fine. Just leave it in your cubby hole before your shift." She walks backwards in the direction of the door to the main cafe. "Give Sam a break once you're done."

I nod at her, willing her to move out of the room faster. As soon as she's out of sight, I rip the ring off my finger. He must have slipped it on while I was asleep—it's the only plausible explanation.

The ring is weighted and solid. It looks and feels more expensive than anything I own. The golden band glints in the light as I bring it closer to my eyes to read the words engraved in his writing:

EVEN IN DEATH

My heartbeat stutters at the words. I've stopped trying to decipher the meaning of the Faceless Man's words, crossing it off as just plain poetry. But those three words hold too much meaning this time after the dream I had and the hours of research on the computer, looking at the meaning of his name.

The inside of the band catches my attention and turns my blood cold:

LETUM & LILITH

Despite the fear, something else shakes me to my core.

He hasn't left me.

He still wants me.

I'm still his muse.

It wasn't a dream.

I know who he is.

I've sat here for five minutes, staring at the ring. If Evan or any of his flatmates saw me sitting in my car outside of their house, no one bothered to check on me.

After my shift finished, I slipped the ring back on without thinking. Like it has always been there and I'm naked without it. The weight is comforting on my finger, a small reminder that he's always with me, even though his mark is already wrapped around my neck.

I used to hate mixing metals; silver and gold. Now it feels like that's how it should be worn, balancing in harmony yet perfectly opposites: love and hate; life and death; heaven and hell.

I glance away from the ring, then back to the text I received from him the second I slipped the ring back on. A single word.

Unknown Sender: Soon.

A shiver rolls down my spine every time I see it, and little bells go off in my head. Not in alarm, but in anticipation.

I know I should take the ring off before going to see Evan. I have to. But it feels like I might lose the Faceless Man forever if I take it off. He only contacted me after gifting the ring, what if I take it off and he goes away again? The ring was the only contact I've had from him in days. Does any of that matter if I'm just here to break up with Evan?

It's been a long time coming. Hearing the same feminine giggle on the other side of the phone every time I spoke to him this week was what made me crack. He's not happy with me, I'm not happy with him. We both have someone else who makes us feel alive while we just go back to each other to poison the well we share. Still, I owe it to him not to wear someone else's ring. The fact that it's on my promise finger is irrelevant right now.

With another ragged breath, I decide to keep it on—just on another finger. Not for any other reason but the fact that it brings me comfort. A reminder that there is someone out there who is looking out for me in their own twisted way. I admit that wearing this might make me a bad person, and no amount of shit Evan's thrown my way makes it any better. If anything, this is a silent '*Fuck you, Evan*'. To add fuel to the fire, Letum will probably like knowing that I'm wearing his ring while breaking up with Evan.

It's worrisome because that very thought makes me tuck my ringless hand into the pocket of my hoodie, while the other is glinting under the gray sky as I make my way inside.

The house is quiet, just as it was when I came here a week ago. I probably should have texted him to make sure that he was home. His truck is in the driveway, but that doesn't really say much, he's never been the type to volunteer to drive. Evan is the type of guy that would rather be in control of the music.

He doesn't work nights like his other two flatmates, and lord knows what that obsidian-haired girl's work hours are like when she seems to be there every time I've spoken to Evan. Well, at least I think that it's her. Unless he has another *friend* that I don't know about.

Nate looks up at me from his spot on the couch when I walk into the living room. He gives me the same pitiful look as last time. It makes me shrink into myself and I twist my new ring for some semblance of comfort.

I clear my throat, not sure if I should say goodbye to him or apologize in advance if I come out screaming.

"Is Evan home?" Can Nate see the fear on my face? Has he noticed that I'm wearing a new ring? Unlikely, but the gold band is at the forefront of my mind, right next to the five words I'm about to say to Evan.

Nate looks at his hands for a moment, a barely visible tremor goes through his jaw. "I heard him busy in his room at lunch. But he's been napping for the whole afternoon."

Busy. Right. Busy gaming? Busy talking to someone that isn't me? Busy using a whole paycheck for drugs? Or busy finding himself in another woman?

I can't get angry when I was dreaming about another man—only it turns out that it might not be a dream after all.

I nod and shuffle my feet over the worn carpet until I reach the first room on my left with the smudges around the handle from opening the door straight after working construction.

Dread sits heavy in my chest. There's a nagging feeling at the back of my head that something bad is going to happen. *You're just working yourself up*, I tell myself. The ring is giving me anxiety just as much as it's giving me comfort.

I hang my head back and stare at the ceiling, trying to muster up all of my confidence and my energy while also mentally preparing myself for whatever venom might spill from his lips. I imagine my Faceless Man standing behind me while whispering words of encouragement, giving me the strength I need to go through with this.

I take a fortifying breath, then knock. When he doesn't respond, I call, "Evan."

Biting the bullet, I grasp the old-fashioned door handle and push the door open slowly, inch by inch. He doesn't stir at the sound, still buried beneath the duvet. So I let myself in and close the door loudly behind me in the hopes that it will wake him.

I'm too anxious to go any further, so I press myself against the door. The idea that I could easily swing it open to run adds some calm to my dire situation.

His room is the same as always. Sort of. Hanging on the back of his chair is a baby blue cardigan, the one that the girl with the obsidian hair was wearing. A two seater green couch is squeezed between the door and his computer setup that's littered with old take-out packets. I zero in on the tube of lipgloss hidden within the mix of rubbish, and the matching baby blue scrunchy hanging off the handle to the closet. I wonder what I'd find if I opened and looked inside. More things that belong to the obsidian girl, perhaps?

What little light that streams in makes the whole situation more gruesome. Like God knows what is about to happen and he's filling the sky with gray clouds just for cinematic effect.

"Evan," I whisper. *Just wake up so we can get this over with, goddamnit.*

He doesn't even stir.

"Evan," I say louder this time.

Nothing.

I force myself to move toward him, clearly needing to shake him awake. Why couldn't this be easy? I'm going to wake him up and he's going to be mad about it and it'll make this whole thing so much worse. I just have to keep telling myself that I need to say those five words, and this can all be over.

When I near the bed, ice rains over my skin from the sight of a rolled-up brown parchment sitting innocently on top of a sleeping Evan.

Has the Faceless Man been sending Evan letters too? No, I doubt it. Evan thought I was insane when I kept saying that he was leaving me notes. Why would Letum leave me a letter at Evan's? I shudder involuntarily from calling him something other than 'the Faceless Man'.

I will my hands to stop shaking as I reach for the letter and try to get my breathing under control. I wouldn't be surprised if Evan woke up just from the sound of my thundering heartbeat.

I can barely unroll the letter with how violently my fingers are shaking. The weight of the ring suddenly feels like it may as well be a boulder. Why did I think a band would bring me comfort when the man who gave it to me sends my anxiety skyrocketing?

Squeezing my eyes shut for a moment, I reopen it to read his note. Then I read it again. And again. All while everything around me comes crashing down. I keep hoping the words will say something different. Keep hoping that it is just my mind playing tricks on me. Each time I reread it, bile creeps higher and higher up my throat.

I slowly reach to move the duvet, hoping what the letter says isn't real. I look up from the letter and stagger back.

"No," I gasp, bringing my hands to my lips to stop from throwing up. "No, no, no, no."

Evan's vacant eyes stare straight at the ceiling, his blue lips are parted ever so slightly, like he's still taking his last breath.

I read the letter one more time.

The fates have not yet called upon his soul. I decided
that he lost it the second he laid his eyes on you.

My heart splinters and shatters and twists. Every atom, every cell, every bit of tissue in me feels like it combusts. My body seizes. And I scream.

CHAPTER SEVEN

LILITH

No.

No, no, no, no, no.

This is all my fault. Everything that's happened. He's dead. Evan's *dead*.

I don't hear Nate thundering through the hallway before the door flings open, slamming against the wall.

"What? What happened? Are you okay?" His frantic eyes are wide, searching the room for an intruder, but he won't find one.

I shove the paper in my pocket before he sees it. "Evan," I sob. I can't get the words to come out of my mouth. If I don't say it, it won't be true. Any second now Evan is going to jump up and say that it was just a practical joke. He won't, though. "He's—" I choke on the words.

Nate gets what I'm trying to say and lunges straight for Evan's body. He immediately pushes his finger against Evan's throat to check for a pulse. He doesn't need to check. I should tell him. Evan is dead. I know that he's dead. Letum killed him.

I can't do anything but watch. I'm stuck. I can't move. Not even shed a tear. All I can do is stare with my breath caught in my throat, burning, aching. I want to scream again—it felt so good to scream.

"Fuck!" Nate yells. He yanks the blankets off and pushes his ear against Evan's still chest. "I—I can't— " He shakes Evan's body before moving his head to Evan's lips. "I can't hear anything. He's not fucking breathing."

He's not breathing, and it's my fault. I should have figured out how to get rid of Letum. I should have turned down his advances. I shouldn't have engaged with him in that stupid dream. I should have left Evan earlier, so he'd still be alive. *I should have. I should have. I should have!*

"Fuck." Nate pushes off the bed and paces, running his hands through his bronze locks and down his face. "*Fuck.* Fucking hell. How—How did this—What—" Nate can't even finish his sentence. He's acting and feeling enough for the both of us.

I'm waiting for my eyes to start stinging or to start gasping for breath. But all I can do is stare. Slowly, the black tendrils in my mind reach for me, pulling me back into the spot where there is no hurt, there is no pain, there is just darkness. In here, I can't hear Nate yelling at me and cursing or screaming that we need to call an ambulance. I don't even see him start CPR.

Evan was an asshole, but he didn't deserve to die. Before the accident, he was perfect, the man of my dreams. Evan was the type of man you'd read about in books, where you'd go home to find the shirt you've been eying up in a bag on the bed. He used to say all of the right things, shower me with affection, he'd try to spend every waking moment touching me. Not sexually, just to remind each other that we are there for one another.

I had planned our wedding: A three-tiered buttercream cake with violet orchid designs. I would have a simple lace dress with shoe-string straps and a short train. We would play Abba while I walked down the aisle, because *Dancing Queen* was playing at the bar the first time we met.

I'll never have the wedding I wanted. Not because Evan's dead now, but because I am. The only difference between the two of us is that I'm still breathing. The only thing that I have to look forward to in my day are letters from my stalker and the flowers he leaves me.

The accident ruined everything. I lost my only remaining family, the job of my dreams and my boyfriend, all in one night.

I told Evan that the Faceless Man was real, and he didn't believe me. He called me crazy and it cost him his life. *I* cost him his life. Will anyone else blame me for his death? Will Letum declare to the heavens that Evan's death was done in my name?

The worst part is, despite the accusations running through my head, I don't truly feel guilty. I only know that I should be. I didn't ask Letum to kill Evan. I can't be at fault for a trigger being pulled when I didn't even know there was a gun. The signs were there—the obsession, the cryptic messages. He never displayed any violence, his touch was tender and soft. Except in that dream, but that was a different situation.

The thing I feel most guilty about is the sense of relief that comes with Evan's death. It hurts that he's dead, but death feels familiar to me. Death itself is sure. It's stable and consistent. You can rely on it happening.

I cried for help. Over and over I begged for help. I begged Evan for support, and he gave me nothing. But it turns out, the only person that helped me was the person I thought I needed saving from. Except, now I realize I needed saving from myself.

Three ominous knocks pull me from the recesses of my mind and it's like coming up for air after being in the water too long. I've heard it before. The knocks. The last two times I was with Evan, we both heard it.

When the fog from my mind clears, Letum is standing in front of me in his pitch-black coat and the drawn hood. Nate is nowhere in sight. His voice sounds from somewhere in the background, stuttering into a phone.

Letum reaches out to me, running his fingers over the curve of my face. Warmth spreads from every spot he touches. The touch is possessive, yet tender. Like he wants to take me down to hell with him, but wants to hold my hand while doing it.

"My beautiful storm," he whispers, continuously caressing my soft skin. The way he says it isn't pitiful or possessive, rather it's a mirror of what I feel: Relief.

He brings his lips down to my forehead to plant a claiming kiss. "You're all mine now."

My breathing goes rampant, the events catching up to me. My hands find purchase with my neck and my chest, rubbing and massaging, trying to get rid of the urge to scream, trying to find the steady breaths that are lost inside of me. Cold burns my skin when the ring touches me, but for some sick reason, I don't want to take it off.

The weight of the letter sitting in my pocket drags me down to the floor and I curl my fingers behind my neck. Rocking back and forth, back and forth, staring at the invisible speck of dust on his perfectly pressed coat.

Letum is kneeling in front of me again, just like he did on the night that I was meant to die. He took Dahlia from me, now he's taken Evan. Why didn't he take me? Why does he still refuse to let me die?

"What did you do to him?" I gasp. I know what he did. It's a stupid question to ask.

Letum smooths a hand down my leg, and the other hand gently tips my chin up. "My darling, everyone dies eventually. The only question is when. I decided that it would be today."

"You killed him because of me!" I choke out before slapping my hand over my mouth so that Nate doesn't hear.

Letum's head tips to the side ever so slightly. "No, my love. I did not *kill* him. I reprieved his body of his soul."

"That's the same fucking thing," I snap.

His touch is so tender compared to my tone as he tucks my hair behind my ear. "The afterlife would not have taken him if it was not his time." Letum's body tenses and I brace myself. "Such a painless death was a kindness, my thunderstorm. Because of you, I did not make him suffer."

Seriously? "Is that meant to make me feel better?"

He sighs, though not impatiently. Letum's forehead touches my own. I know I should back away, but I don't, I can't. "You will come alive, my night monster. I want to see you shine."

"Bullshit."

"What's bullshit?" a voice says from behind me.

I snap my head up to see that it looks like Nate has aged ten years in a manner of ten minutes. Or maybe it has only been ten seconds. He, too, hasn't shed a tear. Though, like me, his hand is trembling at his side, shaking his phone.

He forgets that I said anything at all, and slumps onto the ground next to me and leans his back against the green couch that Evan and I thrifted together for our old apartment. "The ambulance is on its way," he says defeated.

Neither of us says a word to the other. Not when the ambulance arrives. Not once they take Evan's body away.

The paramedics question us, and we both say the same thing: We found him like that. Only I left out the part where I found him with a letter from the Faceless Man that has been stalking me for the past year and a half. It all goes by in a monotonous blur.

I can't feel anything. I've already spent months grieving him. My mind has already pulled me into its clutches, just leaving one foot out just so I hear enough to nod every few seconds.

I didn't even flinch when I told his parents. How could I not flinch? I should be crying with them. I should be screaming as they are. I should be getting in my car and following them to the hospital because after all they think I'm his girlfriend. In reality, the girl with the blue cardigan is closer to him than I am.

Perhaps it's cruel or petty, but I won't be the one to tell her. She clearly sees Evan often enough she'll find out on her own. She still has to come by and pick up her cardigan.

Everything crashes when I make it to my car. Like a livewire, everything in me ignites. The static in my lungs burns as I scream. Pounding fists and palms on the steering wheel, over and over and over until my throat is completely raw, my hands begin to bruise and my arms burn from the pain.

I'm bitter. I'm angry. I'm upset. What is wrong with me that death doesn't want me? Why not me?

I hit the overhead light and ignore the shitty worn seats of my crappy old car, and dig through my bag until I find the familiar orange bottle. There's no point in taking it when Letum is clearly real. But it gives me some peace of mind, a false semblance of calm.

The lid pops open and tumbles down the side of the seat. I curse under my breath but tip a single pill onto the palm of my hand. I never look at it before I take it. For some reason, I do this time.

My grip on the bottle loosens, and it drops onto the car floor, scattering white pills all around. I bring the single pill closer. There's a symbol on it. Not his symbol, *mine.*

A crescent moon with a cross hanging down the bottom: The symbol of Lilith, the she-demon.

The pill drops with the rest of them. How long have they been like this? I only searched up Lilith's symbol the other day. Have I been taking Dr. Mallory's medication at all? No, I must have. I have all the symptoms she warned me about. Did he swap them out?

One by one, I pick up the pills checking to see if they all have the same symbol. *No.* I am *not* crazy. Letum is real. I'm being treated for—I don't even know anymore.

"Letum," I scream, looking out of the window expecting him to be standing under one of the streetlights. I can't see him, but I know he can see me. He's watching. He always is. "What are you doing to me? What the fuck do you want from me?"

I don't know what I expected, but nothing about my surroundings changes.

I scream again before pressing my forehead to the steering wheel to try to regain my composure. Seconds go by, or maybe minutes. I can't be sure how long goes by as I stare at the constellation of pills on the floor of my car.

But I am sure of one thing.

I still want Letum by my side.

I don't recall driving home, but I did. The last thing I remember was twisting the gold ring around my finger. Now, I'm turning my ignition off, my car is parked on the street in front of my apartment. I know that I drove, I just don't think I was conscious while doing it.

My footsteps echo against the groaning wooden staircase as I climb the two stories to my apartment. I fidget with the letter in my pocket. The only evidence of Letum staking claim over Evan's death when my phone chimes again. Whoever it was, tried to call. Evan's mother, Carol, probably. Maybe a doctor. Possibly Evan's flatmates, though Nate can be the messenger. Evan's friends won't contact me, they don't bother with me anymore.

There won't be anything on there of any importance, only messages of pity or people for me to grieve with. I don't want to deal with it. I can't face his parents when I know why their son was taken from them. I can't face them knowing they'll look at me and see that I've evaded death once again.

My hand wraps around the cold metal handle of my apartment door and I angle the key just right to hear the satisfying *click* of the door unlocking. The hinges groan as I swing the door open, only to stop short of closing it again.

Please, no. Not today. I'm not in the mood.

Like a woman gone mad—and I could have truly lost it from everything that has happened—I check the number on my door: 2B.

The sound of my neighbor's door unlocking forces me inside my own apartment, and I can't help but think that this is my punishment for ignoring the calls and not following the ambulance to the hospital.

Candles decorate every corner of the apartment, pulling me back to my dream. This time they're of all shapes and sizes, some on a candelabra, others planted firmly on the floor.

Every inch of the kitchen bench is covered in platters of fruits and crackers, pomegranates and apples, a roasted turkey, potatoes and vegetables, bruschetta and vinaigrette, bottles of red and white wine, all on top of a deep red tablecloth. Another set of fine china is set up for me. The table is straight out of a movie, like a dining room fit to serve a queen.

In place of a TV hangs a painting that was not there when I left for work this morning. Candles and an assortment of flowers all around it like a makeshift shrine.

I stare at the painting, completely transfixed. It is the most phenomenal thing I have ever seen. As well as the most frightening. A cloaked man stands over a sitting woman with long brown hair wearing a dress spun from gold. Every inch of her is the spitting image of me. Down to the butterfly freckles and the soft scar on my lip. Where the man's head should be is pure inky darkness. The Faceless Man. *My* Faceless Man. Letum. It's the type of painting that belongs in a museum, that artists all around the world would talk about for centuries to come.

I turn and take note of the rest of my apartment, following the rose petals that lead to the bedroom. I'm so numb from everything that has happened today that I'm not sure how to react, other than just to stare at it. Dumbfounded.

My foot hangs over the threshold of my room. Scattered across my desk is everything he has ever given me: the letters, a bag, the thriving lily, silk dresses and lace blouses, a crystal flower, an onyx skull, black feathers, the bag of rose petals that I haven't thrown out.

On the bed are some of the items that I thought I had lost. The ones I swore I left it in one place, and the next, gone. The matching charm bracelet that Dahlia and I always wore. The photoframe of me on the day of graduation, holding up my stupid business degree with the biggest smile on my face. A pile of hair ties. My favorite red lace lingerie with black ribbons.

In the middle of all my things, a single brown parchment that reads:

I'm coming for you.

CHAPTER EIGHT

LILITH

WHEN I SLIP BENEATH my sheets, there's no alcohol or medication putting me to sleep. So I toss and turn, my mind a jumble of questions.

I returned all of the things I thought I lost to their rightful places. But the things from Letum remain untouched on my desk. I'm almost proud of them.

No, proud isn't the right word. Comfort isn't strong enough either. Cherished? Wanted? Seeing every single thing laid out like that says something stronger and more meaningful than any of his letters. It's like he's telling me that he's here for me, as he always has been.

The question remains: *why me?* What did I do to garner his attention? What is it about me that has made him obsessed? I do nothing but mope around my apartment, go to work, unload some of my problems on Dr. Mallory, then repeat the dull cycle.

I need to talk to Letum. I deserve answers. If only he would stop hiding, it's not like I haven't figured out he purposely disappeared. He obviously wants me and thought that Evan was in the way.

Eventually, I fall asleep. Just like the last time, I wake up somewhere other than my bedroom. This time I don't ignore the nagging feeling in the back of my head that tells me this isn't just a dream, but something else entirely. Something more, something real.

The velvet blankets tangle around my legs as I move to sit. Like the last dream, the void above me is swirling with shadows, each flicker is another soul being sucked into the void.

Candles are lined around the room, creating a triangle with the bed in the middle. I only just realized that the triangle is almost as large as my bedroom.

Letum dressed me in something just as revealing as last time. Or maybe I dressed myself in it. I pull myself off the bed and wrap the red velvet blanket around me to try and hide as much of me as I can. The black carpet is plush beneath my feet, and I can't help but wiggle my toes before inspecting the room. It's like he's keeping parts of me I thought I lost.

The four walls around me are painted black, hidden behind grand bookcases filled to the brim with an assortment of items: books, skulls, ornaments from all around the world, vases, and more things that I thought I had lost.

There's a picture of me beaming in front of the Trevi fountain when Dahlia and I backpacked through Europe for two months. A poorly made paper plane and crane with my messages on it. The pearl hair clip that I got when I was a little girl. A mug that I made with Dahlia on a Wine and Pottery night. My sunglasses. A little elephant that used to live on my bed and I slept with it every night.

A fireplace simmers calmly between two bookcases, right in front of a chaise flanked by a single-seater wingback couch. There's something about this room that is familiar, I just can't put my finger on why.

My body is so attuned to Letum's physical presence that I know exactly when he materializes behind me.

"You look good in my space." The rumble of his voice casts silken shivers through my body.

I spin around and become caught in his trap. He's wearing the same sleeveless cloak that shows off the mouthwatering curve of his muscles. I didn't get the chance to run my fingers over the ridges the last time. Would he shudder under my touch? Would the marks on his skin recoil from me? Would I be able to feel them?

"I know who you are," I force myself to say. Having practically his entire body on display is too distracting, especially when the sharp 'V' on his stomach is pointing directly to the area that I've been wanting to feel between my legs for longer than I care to admit.

"I did tell you my name." His tone is almost teasing.

I frown. He knows what I meant. "I know *what* you are."

Though I can't see his face, something tells me that he's smiling. "You have solved my riddle?"

He moves forward, and I will my feet to move back, when all they want to do is meet him halfway. So the only choice I have is to stay in place and be at his mercy as always; a place I have come to love. Truthfully, I have always liked being at his mercy a little *too* much.

He doesn't stop until he's less than a foot away from me. His presence is taking the oxygen straight from my lungs and replacing it with the smell of the woods right before a hunter pounces on its prey.

The smooth expanse of his chest is directly in my line of sight, making the need to reach out and touch it even stronger. Up close, the swirling shadows beneath his skin remind me of flames flickering right before wisps of smoke escape into the night. Like a flame, it's warm to be around, but you know it will be scorching to the touch.

"Yes," I mutter and look down at my feet. What if I'm wrong and make a complete fool of myself? I spent time researching what his name meant, and the answer I found was the only thing that has made sense since the accident.

"Look at me, Lilith," he whispers as he tips my chin up to him. My muscles give up the battle for control and the velvet blanket drops and pools around our feet.

"I can't see you." I sound so meek. How could he be interested in someone like me?

"I can see *you*."

There's nothing he has ever said that has been truer. He sees me more than I see myself. Fear bubbles inside me, like maybe if he keeps looking, he'll figure out he does not want me anymore, and that I have nothing to offer.

He leans down and brushes his lips against mine. I breathe in to try and capture his scent, wishing I could stay like this forever. His affection for me oozes from his skin and rains all over me, and everything feels *right*.

He laces his fingers in my hair and our lips collide only to break apart a moment later. "Tell me, my night monster, who am I?"

I suck in my bottom lip before saying, "You are the one who refuses to take my soul. You are Death."

A rumble of approval sounds from his chest as he returns his lips to mine. "Good girl."

My knees almost buckle from the two words. I lean my whole weight against him just to feel him beneath my hands. I'm not sure who makes a move first, but our lips crash against each other and my hands develop a mind of their own, exploring his body, feeling the hard muscles of his back that are hidden under soft skin, wishing that he would just take the goddamn hood off.

Molten heat pools between my legs and I try to pull him even closer, not wanting an inch of space between us.

Letum hums in approval and returns the favor by kicking the velvet blanket away from our feet, stalking forward slowly and pushing me back until I hit the edge of the bed.

His movements become more urgent, kissing my neck like he's waited a lifetime to do it. Despite the hunger in his movements and the hard length pressed against my thigh, his entire body is rigid like there's a beast trapped in his skin, wanting to devour me.

Warm hands ride up my thigh and circle my waist as he devours my neck. "He didn't deserve you." His voice is heavy with lust and burning with rage. The duality does something perverted to my insides, and I almost ask him to say it again until I realize exactly what came out of his mouth.

The words douse the fire, and sober me. He lifts off me because of the slightest pressure I placed on his chest. I just wish I could see his face so I can tell how he's feeling.

"Why did you kill him?" I demand. "It can't just be because I was dating him, I'm sure you would have killed him a long time ago if it were that."

Instead of responding, he drops to his knees between my legs. My breath stutters and my legs widen on instinct. He plants a kiss on the inside of my thigh, and I almost forget the question that I asked.

"I did not kill him," Letum corrects and places another kiss on the opposite thigh. "I do not *kill*. I *take*." His large hands start massaging my thigh, tugging my core closer to the edge of the bed. "However, you are right, my dark love. He was not in my way. I could have taken you whenever I wanted."

Blood rages in my ears from my pounding heart at his words and from his fingers that are slowly lifting the dress up my hips to reveal the wetness he caused. *Death* hums darkly and tears his attention away from his next meal and back to me.

"He laid a hand on you when he shouldn't have. He spoke to you in ways that make me regret taking his soul so peacefully." The lust is gone from his tone. I've never heard him sound so serious. "Given the option again, I would make him scream before I took his soul. The sound would be nothing compared to the noises you will make when I'm inside you."

I squirm under his hands to try and hide the way my traitorous body reacts to such violent words.

Letum reaches for my neck to bring me down to his eye level. My eyes snap to his hands, drinking in the way the muscles in his forearm twitch with each movement. The smoke on his skin doesn't recoil like I thought it would, continuing to dance across his body. I was too distracted last time to pay attention to how the smoke reacts to me.

His fingers tighten around my throat as if he knows that I've been thinking about what they'd look like on me, and he wants to make my wish a reality.

"You're still wearing my necklace." His voice is laced with carnality and possession, and I can't help but lean forward to increase the pressure. Letum rises just enough to pull my bottom lip between his teeth, and a needy whimper leaves me. "I'm going to mark your body and your soul."

I hesitate. "Are you—Are going to take my soul?" Does he hear how hopeful I am? Will he finally accept my offering?

"I already have it." There's no uncertainty in his voice, and I'm not even sure how that might be the case. If there is some way beyond my mortal comprehension where he does, in fact, have my soul, that it's possible for him to have taken it and left me alive; I wouldn't be surprised if he actually does.

Despite the fear that he stirs in me, I have no qualms about letting him take my soul just for himself. Everything about it feels right, like every second of my life has led me to this moment, to him, to us.

"But I want to die." For the first time since the accident, I am uncertain that it's actually what I want. Because what I actually *want* is to be anywhere with the man that has kept me alive for the past year and a half.

He caresses my cheek. "Even death will not keep you from me, my night monster."

"There's nothing I can offer you." I don't know why I'm trying to convince him to stop liking me when I know that it would truly kill me if he did stop.

He rises to his feet from the side of the bed, then occupies the space next to me and pulls me onto his lap as if I were weightless. "*You* are enough, Lilith."

I drop my attention to my hand, picking the skin on the side of my nail. "You don't know anything about me."

His hand covers my own, stopping me from sabotaging myself further.

"Oh, my love," he mutters against my forehead before planting a tender kiss. "I know your hopes and your dreams better than I know myself. I have memorized how the left side of your lips twitches right before you smile. How your eyebrows pinch together and you chew the inside of your cheek while you think. Oh, my sad flower, the sound of your laugh is imprinted into my memory." He starts running his hands through my hair. "I know that your last thought before you sleep is what you might find next to you when you wake up. You pretend to hate it, but you secretly like working at the cafe because you love being surrounded by life. The wounds you wear run deeper than your scars from that night. The guilt you harbor over being the one to live."

I can feel him looking down on me, but I can't bring myself to look up. He has been watching me for a year and a half, of course he knows.

"I know nothing about you." He apparently knows so much about me but I know practically nothing about him.

He pulls me closer and tucks my head between his collar and jaw. "You know everything about me, my love. You just keep it locked away."

"I don't," I object. "I don't know your favorite season, what type of music you like, what time of day you prefer, what you actually look like, your hobby, your favorite thing to eat." Does Death need to eat? Sleep? How does he have all this time to follow me around if he needs to collect souls—or whatever he does?

Letum's arms disappear from me, and the chill from the absence of his touch strikes me to my core. He deposits me back on the edge of the bed. I'm about to stand to look at him, just so he knows that even though he has me on his hook, I'm still not just going to stay there, but he wraps his arms around my waist before I can and pulls me up the bed with him.

He molds our bodies together as if we have done this a thousand times. He knows just how perfectly we fit together. His hard length presses against my ass, and it takes more strength than I care to admit not to grind my hips.

"Autumn. Classical. Right before the sun rises. You, and you." My core tightens when he starts skimming the tips of his fingers across my stomach.

A blush heats my cheeks. I should have guessed his favorite season would be autumn, after all it's the time when life seeps away from nature. "You didn't say what you look like."

His chest vibrates against my back with his warm chuckle and he kisses the side of my neck. It could be my mind hearing what it wants, but he almost sounds proud of me for noticing. "I will answer any question that you ask. But *that*, you will need to discover for yourself."

Taking it as an invitation, I unwind our tangled legs and force our bodies apart. Will his cheekbones be high or low or right in the middle? Is his jaw as sharp as his body, or will there be an almost boyish look to him?

Slowly, I reach for his hood, as if any sudden movements might scare him away. He brings my hand to his lips before I even touch the soft material, and grazes his lips along my knuckles and tsks. "You can see once you open your eyes."

Seeds of frustration plant their roots and blossom. "They're open," I snap. I didn't stand up for myself when Evan gaslit me, yet I'm inches away from biting the hand that has been keeping me above water.

"Not yet, my love, but they will be soon."

I almost push away from his hold. What the hell is that supposed to mean? He keeps saying 'soon'. I truly don't believe he's ever lied to me, though the non-answers are starting to feel so much worse. This is probably another thing that he wants me to do for myself, just as he has been coaxing me to voice my needs and wants.

Is it because this is basically a dream? Or is he just hiding from me? Or is he as insecure as I am?

I try escaping his hold on my wrist, but he doesn't budge. Instead, my free hand travels up his stomach and on top of where his heart should be. Except nothing beats beneath my hand.

"Letum." His name feels so good wrapped around my tongue. Does he think so too? "I don't care what you look like. If you're scarred or truly faceless."

He hums, sending ripples up my arms and to my heavily beating heart. "And what is it that you care about, my dark love?"

You.

It's on the tip of my tongue to say it, but I refuse to let the one syllable out. Not when he's still hiding so much from me. So I change the topic.

"What happens to souls when they die?"

I think I feel him smile. "I walk them to the gates of the afterlife, and what happens after is the soul's choosing." He nips my finger. "If they believe in heaven and hell, then that is the path the soul will follow. If they believe in nothingness, then eternal slumber awaits. If they believe in reincarnation then you will find them again on this earth, in this lifetime, or the next."

What do I believe? If I believe that I will walk the afterlife beside Death, is that what will happen?

What did my parents believe? They weren't overtly religious, though they didn't dispel the idea of god with a capital 'G' or otherwise. Dahlia once said that she would be reincarnated into a rich person's handbag dog, but I don't know how much truth is in that.

As if reading my thoughts, he says, "I do not know where the souls of your family are, my love."

"Oh," I mutter and drop my attention back to my hands. I frown. "Why do you leave those symbols on me?"

He lets go of my hand and wraps his arms around me to pull me to him, where we cuddle like real lovers. Out of pure instinct, I burrow my head against his chest and slide my hands beneath his cloak to roam his back as if it were muscle memory.

His scent washes over me and with it the feeling of peace. In my life, I've never felt so calm and content. I could stay like this for eternity and never long to see the light of day. How could someone I know so little about make me want to give him everything short of the moon and the stars?

"So when you wake up, you remember me," he replies.

I suck in a sharp breath and debate whether to change the topic again so I don't need to admit the truth. After a moment of hesitation, I say, "I've never forgotten about you."

"And you never will."

"How can you be so sure?"

His fingers trail love notes along my back. "I have waited a lifetime for you, my Lilith. I am not letting you go."

My hands move on their own accord, descending down his back to the top of his pants. I crook a finger into the band and follow the path to the front of him. His length hardens and pushes into my stomach as he takes a staggering breath.

My arousal pools low in my stomach knowing I have such a profound effect on him, just like he does on me.

I pinch the strings of his breeches, a second away from tugging it when he stops my movements once more. "Not tonight, my love. We will have all of eternity to explore each other's bodies. *Tonight,* you need to be held."

"Please," I beg.

He tenses but doesn't let go. The silence makes me wild with need. I need his hard length to sit heavy in my hands or hit the back of my throat until I see stars. I need to be filled by him so thoroughly that there will be no room in my mind for anything other than him. I need to feel alive. He doesn't even need to let go of me. There doesn't need to be a breath of space between us for him to bury himself in me.

What would Dahlia say if she knew that I'm begging Death himself to fuck me hours after he took Evan's soul? Regardless of what she might think, I can't bring myself to care. Nothing else matters but Letum and I.

"*Please,*" I whimper.

A warning growl thunders low in his throat. "*Fuck*, Lilith. You don't understand, do you?"

Liquid fire douses my skin and I writhe beneath him, my arousal hot in the air and the space between us is heavy with our aching needs. "What?" I gasp.

If he knew the state of what is happening between my legs, I'm sure there would be no more talking going on between us. This is one of the few chances I have to get to know him, and all I want is to feel him inside of me. What does that say of me?

He slams his lips to mine and devours me in an earth shattering kiss. Still, his hands stay wrapped around my waist. "You command me. Not just my heart—*all of me.*"

I drag my teeth down his lip before he gets the chance to break the kiss. "Please, Letum. I just want to feel."

Before I can blink, his weight is on top of me and his fingers disappear down to my aching core. "Fuck," he snarls, pushing his fingers through my heat. "You're so wet for me, my love."

I watch with bated breath as he pulls away from my center and brings his hand into the space between us. Light glistens off his wet fingers and he grumbles in approval as he tastes me once again. "Yes," he says, low and heated. "You are my favorite thing to eat."

Oh god.

"Don't stop," I beg.

He devours me in another kiss, the taste of me still sweet on his tongue. Strong fingers delicately strum my clit like he already knows how to make me sing. He swallows my cry and balances himself on an elbow before gripping my throat possessively.

"My love," he says breathlessly. "You're fucking magnificent when you use your words. Do you know what happens when you're good?"

I try to stop myself from closing my eyes and lose myself in the feeling as he circles my clit with expert precision and I almost forget how empty I feel without him inside me. "What—"

I gasp when his fingers curl inside of me, hitting the right spot instantly. "You get rewarded."

Thick fingers pump in and out of me, not stretching me as much as he did last week, but no less euphoric. I arch my back to his touch as his hand squeezes around my throat, slowly stealing even more of my breath and quieting my moans. Would it be wrong to ask if his shadow can join?

Little by little, oxygen becomes a commodity rather than a necessity, burning my lungs with pleasurable heat.

"Do you want to come?"

I nod my head as much as his grip allows it, pushing my thighs further apart to take even more of him. My eyelids drift shut of their own accord as my body becomes as light as air.

"You know what you need to use."

My words.

"I want to come." The words are barely a whisper, but the gasp of a woman about to die in bliss.

His pumps become more brutal, hitting the spot that makes stars explode. "Then come alive for me."

His thumb swirls the spot that is dying for friction. Every morsel of my being fractures and collapses as my orgasm tears through me. Air rushes into me like wildfire as I gasp hungrily for breath, attempting to ride out the climax when he doesn't relent with his assault.

I scream and curse, begging him to stop as electricity sparks through my system like a livewire. Just when I think I can breathe again, he drops to his stomach between my thighs and laps up the mess that I made.

He pulls my clit between his teeth and plunges his fingers back inside of me.

"Shit, shit, shit, shit." I chant as my body and mind fails to comprehend a single thing.

Oh god, he's going to kill me if he doesn't stop.

I buckle and try to reach beneath Letum's hood to grab onto his hair, but he stops me in a death grip, holding me down as he licks me clean. The sounds of his approval and lust vibrate through my sensitive core, forcing another sky splitting scream.

He removes his fingers and settles his weight on top of me, rubbing the remnants of my desire along my lips.

"Taste what I taste," he orders.

I'm too delirious to do anything but comply, flicking my tongue out and licking myself clean off his fingers. Then I notice a gold band around his finger, the same thickness and inscription as the one he's given me, even wearing it on the same finger.

"You are mine, Lilith. You belong to me."

CHAPTER NINE

LILITH

IT HAS BEEN THREE days since Letum took Evan. During that time, his parents managed to throw together a funeral, and I have barely left my bed. Until now. Where death hangs in the air of the church, but not *my Death*.

Guilt strapped me to the sheets. Not for what I'm *meant* to be guilty about. Evan's blood is on my hands. I live, and he doesn't.

What would have happened if I didn't sit in the middle seat of the car that night? What if I had sat behind the driver's seat like I usually do? It was out of character for me to sit in the middle seat because I hated how hard the cushioning always was. I always thought I saw too much when I sat in the middle. For some reason, that night, out of all the nights, I had the urge to sit in the middle.

The voice in the back of my head says that it was fate. So that I could meet Letum. But I'm not sure if that voice is only saying it because I haven't had a single pill since Evan died.

My mom used to say that it was fate that I got a job before I even graduated. She said that it was fate when she was diagnosed with stage four bowel cancer a month after my father died from it. She'd say that fate was good to her and gave her twins so that Dahlia and I would never be alone.

Fuck fate. I want to spit and rage at how unfair it all is.

I wonder if the obsidian-haired girl thinks that it's fate that she found a man only to lose him. I overheard her tell Carol, Evan's mom, that she was close with her son. *Olivia*, she called herself. They sobbed into each other's arms like old friends. The obsidian-haired woman—*Olivia*—isn't wearing a blue cardigan this time, but a tight fitted black dress. Evan would have loved that dress.

I watch her from my spot next to the bathroom door. People file in and offer their condolences, all while she stands next to the family like she's the one who held the title of 'the girlfriend'. As far as I know, maybe she did to everyone else but me and Evan's parents.

Does standing where I should be standing help her grieve? She hasn't had the months that I've had to mourn him, so I'm sure the only thing to call myself is lucky. And cursed.

Some people nod at me, some give me the same pitiful look that I haven't stopped seeing since the accident. When Nate looks at me, guilt isn't hidden underneath the pity; it's only pity this time. He knew what Evan was doing and didn't tell me. He heard Evan call me crazy. Look at where we are now.

The rest of Evan's flatmates file in behind Nate. They all knew, and they said nothing. Each one of their backs straightens or tenses when they see Olivia with the family, and me alone in the corner. They smile meekly at me before rushing to take their place inside the church Evan had no faith in.

No one has mentioned the elephant in the room: that he died of an overdose. Every third person would say something along the lines of how he was so filled with life and that he was such an exemplary young man.

Exemplary implies that he wouldn't touch drugs. *Exemplary* implies that he wouldn't gaslight his 'girlfriend'.

He was *exemplary* in his earlier days. The accident made him wicked—no, not wicked, *broken*. Evan was my anchor, except the rope was too short and it kept me drowning below the surface. Now the rope has been cut, and in time, my body will decompose and float to the surface. Whether that's scientifically possible, I'm not sure. Science stopped having meaning when Death came into my life.

Earlier, Carol had come up to me and said, "It must be so hard. Losing your whole family, then the man you were going to start a family with."

I bit my tongue and smiled at her because there was nothing I could say. The truth of what her son was like was on the tip of my tongue, but I decided to keep my awfulness to myself. Everyone can mourn and grieve alongside their last memory of Evan. I will too, except, my grief doesn't feel like pain; it feels like freedom.

I lean against the wall for support as a brain zap renders me momentarily useless. The nausea spells started this morning. I don't need Dr. Mallory to tell me what the side effects of going off my medication are, especially when I didn't wean myself off it but instead, stopped taking them completely. *Cold turkey*, as they call it.

The service starts, and everyone still in the foyer takes their place along one of the many pews. Just like the night of the accident, I get a feeling to stay behind and wait in the foyer.

Goosebumps blanket my skin as the music starts, and the comforting smell of the sea trickles into my soul. I'm not sure what hurts more, that Evan is dead, or that Letum has not made contact since I came undone on his fingers. Again.

When I spin around, my stomach sinks.

He's not there. Instead, I swear I see Dahlia in the corner of my vision. When I turn, she isn't there.

I clutch my phone tightly as I pull up our message thread.

Me: Where are you?

I stare at my phone, waiting for a reply that won't come.

Swallowing the hurt, I force my legs to move and carry me to a pew where I mourn for a man who I have already finished grieving. As I stare at the coffin before the lectern, I yearn for the man who did not want to take my soul.

My apartment is a prison with unlocked doors. I don't want to step beyond the bars and succumb to the mundane cycle of a meaningless life.

Each morning I wake up hoping to find a brown parchment tucked next to my head, but there's none. Despite the pain, I still force myself to go to work.

Two weeks. *Two*. Not a single letter saying that he's heading out of town for a bit or there's an influx of souls to collect. *Nothing*. Not even a stupid flower.

Letum said that he will never let me go. He didn't say that it was because I would be latching on to him. Why am I mourning the loss of Letum who *is* Death, rather than Evan, who is *dead*?

I haven't taken any of Dr. Mallory's medication since the day Evan died. At first, it was just because I wasn't sure whether Letum swapped out the pills. Then it was because I thought I might be able to see him in my dreams. After, I didn't have a choice because all of the bottles disappeared.

Death's doing, I assume.

So, he can take the medication keeping my emotions at bay, and at the same time take the one thing that was actually keeping me sane.

When I need him the most.

I grip the counter as another brain zap rattles me, making me tense and relax at the same time. Hopefully, no one noticed.

I had no choice but to call in sick the first week and a half after the funeral. The withdrawals were hitting me like a ton of bricks, and I found myself hurling over the toilet with nothing coming out, and laying in bed partially comatose as another brain zap paralyzed me momentarily.

Without pay and without Letum's financial contributions, I can't afford to buy the medications again. Letum's remaining cash has acted as a buffer, which means that I can still afford rent, electricity, and food, if I actually go out to buy some. So at least there's that to be grateful for.

Out of the corner of my eye, I spot Brit giving me another look of pity. All of my coworkers have. I'm so sick of everyone looking at me like I'm broken. I've heard them talking about how I've lost everyone. I have no family to speak of and no man to warm my sheets. Not like Evan warmed my sheets before he died.

The day progresses like every other: with me suffering through my shift while my locker remains empty and my apartment stays death free.

Letum has cursed me in more ways than one because now I can't resort to the recesses of my mind to escape. Now, tears don't just gather in my eyes, they fall and they don't stop falling. Every night my pillow dampens as I sob into it, thinking that it might take the pain away. Every night, my cries grow louder as if Letum might hear me and decide to come back.

He doesn't. He never does. I'm beginning to think he never will.

When I fall asleep, he doesn't visit me in my dreams despite my calls. Instead, I'm tortured by the memory of the crash. The memory of losing my sister.

I thought I was broken before, but now I feel as if I am breaking all over again. Piece by piece, another shard crumbles away from me. I'm haunted by the jarring realization that this is what it feels like to be well and truly alone.

CHAPTER TEN

LETUM

She thinks that I left her.

I could *never* leave her.

She thinks that I discarded her from my life.

I would sooner walk myself into the afterlife than do that.

Every night for the past three weeks, I sit at the foot of her bed and watch her tears seep into her pillow. She clutches it to her chest as her heart spills onto the floor, flooding the night with her sorrows. It is the most vicious battle, sitting and watching. I have to stop myself from pulling the pillow away and be the one that she clutches onto so her tears can soak into *my* soul.

My undead heart splinters every time I see her. My beautiful night monster's eyes are filled with pain and longing, no longer the empty void that she disappeared into.

It's too much to watch her wither the way she is, but I know it's necessary. She needs to overcome this for the both of us to know she accepts me fully and completely. Her eyes need to open and she needs to remember. It is the only way for us to move forward.

I want to be enough for her in every way. I will be. She will want for nothing and live an eternity by my side. My Lilith will never be alone again because we will be by each other's side forever. My perfect other. My night monster.

Unable to stand by and see her in misery, I continue to write to her. Promising I will never leave her, reminding her of her strength and her beauty. She hasn't noticed her kitchen cupboards haven't emptied, even though she hasn't gone to the store in three weeks. Nor has she noticed she hasn't needed to clean her apartment once.

I told myself I would leave her alone to heal, but I am a weak man.

She does not truly understand the magnitude of her hold on me. She weakens every single part of me and makes me want to be something other than just *death*.

Lilith takes a deep breath, slumped over the steering wheel as she lets a lone tear roll. She has shed at least a single tear at work every day for the past three days. Lilith may be my greatest weakness, but her tears will be what kills Death itself. I always have to stop myself from wiping it away, to kiss her senseless until she forgets about the future, past and present. Until all she can think about is me.

I want my storm to be more than just clouds. I want her to be lightning that splits trees. She will be the thunder that follows too, shaking houses and making children scream in their beds. She is named after the Mother of Demons; she will do nothing short of prosper.

Lilith wipes the lone tear from her cheek and sits up straighter in her seat. She juts her chin out as if she's pretending that she hadn't just cried.

My lily is starting to bloom. It's the most wondrous sight.

The engine rumbles to life, and I watch from the passenger seat as she pulls out of her work car park and heads in the opposite direction of home.

"Where are you going, my night monster?" I say, even though she won't hear.

Buildings peter out and change into pine trees and untamed bushes. Minutes fly past as we head further away from the city, until she slows down and makes a turn for the cemetery.

Oh. The little flower has come to say her goodbyes.

She turns the ignition off but doesn't step out of the car, just stares ahead like she's questioning her decision. I ghost a caress over her cheek in a vain attempt to will her to do what she needs to do.

I will wait a lifetime for her. That does not mean that I am against claiming her sooner rather than later.

My midnight storm twists the ring I gave her and tugs at the necklace like she's making sure it's still there. I cannot discern what she feels when she looks at it; whether she sees it as a strength or a weakness.

The car groans as she pushes the door open and marches toward the graves hidden behind the line of trees. Since she woke up from her coma, she has not stepped foot in Millyard Cemetery. She never said her goodbyes to her sister or visited her parents' grave. When Evan died, she refused to follow the hearse to his final resting place.

Lilith holds her head up as she steps over fallen leaves, sniffling softly, she makes her way over to the three headstones. She ignores the wet grass and falls onto the ground between her mother and sister. I lower myself down onto the ground in front of her.

Birds chirp on surrounding headstones, filling the silence. Her lips twist like she's trying to find the right words.

"Hey," she whispers. Silence hangs in the air as a thousand words string behind her eyes. "It's been a while." She huffs out a laugh as she stares at the ground and shakes her head. "It's not like I've been busy, I've—" she looks up and blinks back tears "—I've just been going through a lot."

The earth around vibrates, and stoic silence blankets the cemetery. The gates to the afterlife have opened to let the spirits beyond hear her.

"Your family is here, my love. Say as much or as little as you want."

She crosses her legs, unaware that she's gathered an audience. "I'm sorry I didn't visit sooner." Giving up the fight, she lets the tears stream freely down her face as she picks at the skin around her nails. "There's no valid excuse I could give you. And I'm so sorry. I know you wouldn't be disappointed in me. It just—" she chokes on a sob. "It hurts so fucking much."

"Since I woke up in the hospital, I haven't let myself feel the pain of your loss. I've mourned it. Grieved it. But I never felt it. And now that I do, I can't breathe." Her entire body shakes. It just shatters me. I need to hold her, I need her to know that I'm right here and she isn't doing this alone. But this is one of the reasons I've had to stand back. She has to do this alone. "I can't fucking breathe knowing you're gone. You're never coming back. And I hate it."

She wipes her tears with the back of her hand and leans her forehead against Dahlia's tombstone. "I miss you so fucking much and I haven't been complete without you. I tried to get back to you. I really did. I tried so hard, Dahl. Even though I knew that isn't what you wanted. I wasn't ready to say goodbye. You kept showing up at the edge of my vision. And I know that it's because you need to say goodbye just as much as I do." Tears stream into her mouth but she doesn't wipe them away. "I didn't want to accept that you were gone forever. I knew you weren't alive, but I was chasing this dream that we would be reunited, and that was the only way I'd get my happily ever after. But the truth is, it's not the ending that I need."

My flower isn't just blooming, she's blossoming. Immense pride and joy cuts at my sadness. We'll be together soon.

"You, mom, and dad would want me to live. But I can't just do that. I can't just *live* and move on and forget about you. I'm sorry, but I just can't." She shakes her head. "Instead, for you, I'll survive." Lilith rakes her fingers through her hair and huffs out an exhausted breath. "I'll survive in my own way. I'll grow, I don't know how just yet. But I will, I promise you."

I eye her curiously as she tugs off the golden ring. She stares at it for a long moment until her tears dry up and the sun is about to set. The faintest smile paints her lips. I want to capture the sparkle in her eye and place it where the sun should be.

"Dahl, I met someone." She chuckles as if her sister is right next to her, alive and well. "Well, he met *me* actually. You've met him too." She uncrosses her legs and leans back against the headstone. Her eyes shine brighter than I've seen before. "Questionable morals, but I think you'd actually like him. The way into your heart was always to get you pretty things, and he does so plenty."

Her soft smile fades slightly, but still, she speaks as if she is talking to a friend. "Oh, and Evan died. That guy I was just telling you about took him. I was mad at first, but now I realize that death is the natural progression of life." Lilith sighs. "Evan ended up being a dick, which isn't the point. The accident broke him too."

The sun dips below the horizon, and still, she continues talking to her sister, telling her what has happened to their friends, about working at the cafe and her little apartment and what it's like to live a life without her other half.

When the moon is the only light guiding her path, she kisses the top of all three tombstones, then heads back to the car.

I told myself that I would wait at least a month for her. It's been three weeks and she isn't ready yet, her soul is still blocked.

She needs room to grow and to heal. But I made my dark love a promise: she gets rewarded when she's good.

And I am nothing, if not a man of my word.

CHAPTER ELEVEN

LILITH

AFTER OVER A YEAR of therapy, that was the first time I've ever felt better after talking. There was no way I would have been able to do it sooner because I wasn't ready to accept the past.

The truth is that I survived. Whether I wanted to or not. Even if the only reason I've survived this long was because Letum did not want to take me, the fact remains that I'm alive. *Living* is another question entirely.

My body feels weightless as I climb up the stairs to my apartment. The worst of the medication withdrawals have passed, and I've been getting the brain zaps once a day at most.

I wasn't sure what was worse, feeling everything or feeling nothing at all. I realize now that I may as well ask if I would rather see everything or nothing, to be told the truth or to be lied to. The preference will always be the aversion to harm. Living in a delusion will only put a plaster on my wounds, not heal them.

My apartment is dark when I step inside, and my stomach grumbles. I sigh the weight of a thousand breaths as I go through the motions of eating a meal that I'll probably just swallow without tasting.

The upholstered wooden stool groans when I put my weight on it, and I almost fall off it when I shift. I twist the spaghetti around my fork and lift it in the air to cool it down. My brows knit together as a barely audible sound drifts through the apartment.

I squint before closing my eyes to determine what the sound is. It almost sounds like... moaning?

The stool squeals against the wooden floor, and the cushioned part swivels as I push back from the seat and try to locate the sound. It's coming from my apartment somewhere.

My nails mark crescent moons into my palm as I follow the sound to my bedroom with hesitant steps. The closer I get, the more certain I am that it's definitely the sound of a woman moaning.

My sappy heart skips a beat at the thought that Letum might have left me something. Even if it's a messed up gift. I try to shake the feeling off when I am supposed to be mad at him for abandoning me. I hate admitting it, but leaving me alone to force me to face my own emotions was the best thing he could have done for me. I wouldn't have been able to see Dahlia and my parents if he hadn't.

Artificial gray light shines through my room from the desk, right where the sound of the moans is coming from. Did I get hacked and get a porn pop-up? No, that can't be right. I haven't used the laptop in awhile.

I inch closer in an attempt to peer over the office chair. At first, the video is grainy like it was recorded with an old-school camera. Then I make out the shapes in the video; matching white bedside tables with one handle missing, thrifted touch lamps that don't match on either side of the bed, a slatted wooden headboard and crisp white sheets with a green duvet bunched at the feet.

I've seen this bedroom hundreds of times.

It's *my* bedroom. The moaning is coming from *me*. From the nanny cam.

In the video, my arms are slack above my head on the bed, and I'm moaning as I grind my hips. "Letum!" I scream in the video as my entire body buckles. But no one else is on the screen.

It's time stamped the same night I dreamt about Letum in a forest.

The video flickers and I'm on my hands and knees with my mouth wide open, making gagging noises as my body is jolted forward like invisible fingers were thrusting into me. Because they were. Letum's soul was.

This whole time it was him. *He* cut the recording straight from the nanny cam and kept it. Oh god. There must be hundreds of hours of footage that he's kept of me. Or maybe of him, of us.

Heat pours through my veins at the memory of that night. Did he rewatch the videos to get off on it? God, what if there are dreams that I don't remember?

My heart skips a beat when I spot a rolled-up brown parchment next to the laptop. Three weeks of no communication or letters. And he chose today of all days to make contact?

I waste no time snatching the letter from the table and unrolling it like my life depends on it.

> *How I long for the taste of the night. How I long to hear*
> *the sound of the storm. I'm coming for you, my love.*

Once I take a bite, you're mine until even eternity comes
to an end.

The arousal pooling between my legs only grows. I try to act like the note doesn't affect me, but I rush back to the kitchen to scarf down my dinner, forgetting all about the fact that he hasn't contacted me in weeks.

Will I see him in my dreams tonight? Will the shadow come out?

I'm consumed with the thought of what might happen when I sleep and the headiness of the words "I'm coming for you." He's said it before, and every time it feels like a promise. This time it's like a countdown.

Bedtime can't come soon enough as excitement pumps through my veins, making me rush to go to sleep as fast I can. I haven't felt giddy in so long, I've forgotten what it feels like.

The shower runs cold for the first thirty seconds, then it slowly heats. It's not a particularly small shower, but it could easily fit two people. Not that I've ever found out if it does.

Hot water cascades down my body, soothing my tired muscles. The pulse between my legs aches as I remember the video and the night it was taken. Does he think about it as much as I do? What else could that shadow do to me? I know I should be angry because it's an invasion of my privacy, but all it's doing is making me flustered.

My hand skates over my heated skin and finds the place that's begging for relief. I bite my lip as I circle the sensitive flesh. I'm getting far too impatient to wait until I sleep, and I can't bear the thought that nothing will happen in my dream tonight.

My breath hiccups when I slip a finger inside of me, imagining it is one of his. Or his shadow's, I'm not picky.

Awareness prickles at the back of my neck a split second before I'm pressed against the wall. The chill of the tile bites my aching nipples and sends sparks down to my core. I gasp in the steaming air and soak in the scent of morning dew.

Letum's fingers thread through my hair, keeping my gaze fixed on the white tile. He doesn't hesitate when he reaches around me and plunges his fingers into me. Pleasure pummels through me, and I scream, throwing my head back onto his shoulder.

"How I've missed you, my love," he grinds out against the shell of my ear. He sinks himself deeper, making my entire body shudder. "There's nothing like home."

How can he think that someone riddled with scars is home? How does he not see me and recoil? Instead, Death's engorged cock presses against my ass without a whisper of material between us. Perhaps in his eyes, I don't have any scars, or maybe I do, and he thinks that they, too, are beautiful.

I try to shift my hips up without losing the mind numbing pleasure his fingers are bringing me, and I wedge my arm out from underneath me to bring it up to feel if he's wearing a hood as well.

He lets go of my hair to land a brutal slap on my ass. The welts that form sends my blood racing every time his thigh brushes against me.

"You have not left my mind for a single second." He pushes his hips against mine, making me feel every inch of his hard length against my burning skin. "I am completely at your mercy, Lilith."

Sweat mingles in with the hot shower water, and I blink away the steam as I reach out to turn the water off.

Another little whimper echoes through the bathroom when he rubs my clit with his thumb and forces another cry from my lips. "Fuck, has your cunt missed the feel of my fingers?"

"Yes, yes. Fuck, yes," I pant. Pressure builds in my core as my climax sprints toward me.

"Do you want me to stop?"

I shake my head so vigorously I almost knock my head against his. My legs buckle, and he keeps me held up by the fist in my hair while his fingers force an orgasm out of me.

"I need to hear you say the words, my love." His fingers work faster, hitting the spot every single time. My core tightens on the brink of an orgasm.

"Please. For the love of god, please don't stop," I beg.

He stops. His fingers disappear from inside me, and I almost scream in frustration.

"You aren't going to come on my fingers," he says with a mischievous lilt in his voice.

My protests die on my lips when his cock teases my entrance from behind, his body pressed against my back. He grips my hips to hold me steady and fills me with a single thrust. The sound of his snarl breaks through my scream as pain lances my core from the sheer girth of him. He pauses as if relishing in the feel of me, sliding deeper, inch by brutal inch. When I think there's nothing left for him to give, he fills me even more. My body stretches to try and accommodate his size. The only thing that prepared me for his size was his shadow's fingers, and it doesn't compare to finally having him inside me.

He did as he promised: he claimed me when I least expected it.

"You are going to come on my cock tonight, my love, and you are going to scream my name when you do it."

My hold on the wall keeps slipping, and I have no choice but to drop my cheek onto the tile and let the stars dance behind my vision while a supernova starts in my core.

His grip leaves my hair, and he holds the tile wall next to my head for support. I'm forced to stare at his straining forearms. Somehow, I'm getting even wetter at the sight of the ticking veins in his hands.

He pummels into me to the point that I can't even hold my own weight. With each thrust he goes a little bit deeper. The tile beneath his hand cracks with the force of his brutal fucking. Despite how vicious his thrusts are, he's still holding back.

I don't remember my own name. I don't know where I am. But I'll never forget his name. I could never forget what he's done to me.

My orgasm thunders through me like lighting, setting every edge of me alight and making me lose feelings in my toes. He doesn't relent with his pounding, squeezing me of everything I have to give and deeming it not enough.

"I'm not done with you yet," he growls in my ear. He shifts his hold on my waist and presses the tip of his finger into the tight ring of my muscle. "Do you want me to stop, love?" he pants without pause in his pounding. "If you want me to fill your ass, you have to say it."

I meet him at his next thrust, taking every single inch of him like I need him just as much as he needs me. His movements slow, sliding into me with more brutal thrusts that stirs pleasurable pain in my core. More heat pools between my legs, encouraging him to tease me with the achingly slow rhythm.

Then he resumes his tortuous pace of pummeling into the wall. He snarls as I whip my head back close to my shoulder blades, arching my back to take even more of him. I used to be well versed in anal toys and having my ass fucked but he doesn't need to know that. Still, Letum's care warms my heart almost as hot as my blood.

"Put it in me," I hiss.

"*Fuck.*" He shoves his fingers into my mouth, pulling my head to him by the cheek. "Get my fingers as wet as you can, love. Because I'll be fucking your ass with them, and then with my cock."

I moan from his words alone. He shoves his fingers all the way until I choke on them. My eyes roll back as he fucks my mouth just as viciously as he fucks my cunt. Unbridled excitement has me sucking his fingers as if they were his cock, and the thought of tasting him on my tongue again causes another orgasm to approach.

"You're a sight to behold," he gasps.

Without warning, he yanks the shower curtain open, breaking the metal rod from off the wall in the process. He pulls out of me, leaving me hollow and empty. His fingers continue to warm my mouth, pulling at my cheek as he guides me forward with a fist in my hair. My head is pushed down to the sink and Letum kills the lights before I get the chance to look into the mirror to see if there is anything concealing his face.

"I'm going to ruin you, Lilith," he says as he pushes a finger into the taut ring of muscle and groans. "So fucking tight."

A breathy moan escapes my lips as he starts working me, getting me ready to take another finger. I'm screaming bloody murder by the time the third goes in.

My core tightens with the need to be filled again. I push my hips back, trying to signal to him to sink into me, but he doesn't heed. My hands travel down to my entrance, and he objects with another slap to my ass.

Goosebumps scatter all over me as the bathroom darkens even more. "I know how much you loved having an extra pair of hands worship you. How would you feel with an extra cock to fuck you with?"

Jesus christ. Of course the man who deals in souls has a dick on his actual soul. If his fingers weren't stretching me so thoroughly, I would be giggling right now.

A cool finger presses against my core for a second, taunting me.

Letum pulls me upright, ushering me out of the door, and makes me miss the chance to see him in the mirror. I try to angle my head to see his face, but his hold on my hair keeps me looking straight ahead.

I try to make out the shape of Letum's soul which occupies almost the whole bed. He isn't as big as he was in the woods, like he's managed to shrink in size. As my gaze travels down what I assume is his waist, anticipation bubbles through my veins. I can barely make out the shape of the soul's hard cock.

Letum kills the lights again and pushes me forward until I'm on the bed, straddling the shadow. He angles me so that I'm just on top of the soul's length. The only lighting there is from the hallway, so I can't see what it is that's about to go inside me. More specifically, how big it is.

I groan as the tip pushes into my core. "It's not going to fit."

"It will," Letum assures as he reaches and rubs my clit. "I know it will."

His soul takes charge of kneading my breasts like they're the most beautiful things he's ever seen. It's invigorating, never knowing the soul's next move and whether he'll bring me pleasure or pain.

His soul places a firm hand on my hip, lowering me further down. I fall forward onto the shadow's chest, bewildered by the fact that I can't see the soul at all and just the blankets beneath him.

Letum's strokes on my clit become more precise, shorter. Sharper. My impending orgasm shatters through me, and I spasm around him. Just as he planned, the muscles in my core relax, letting me drop further down.

Inch by blissful and painful inch, I moan as I stretch more than I thought was humanly possible.

The world around me disappears, and all I can focus on is the fact that he's finally taking me. Slowly, I ride back up his length just to drop back down as low as I can take him. With every descent, I take more of him. Just when I think that I've done all the stretching I can possibly do, the tip of Letum's cock pushes against my other opening.

"I'm claiming every inch of your mortal body. Next, I'm claiming your soul," Letum growls before taking my ass just as he promised he would.

Blood rushes from my head. His intrusion stings, but I've never felt so full. My eyes close and the feeling of being stretched and filled intensifies.

At once, they start their slow movements that will make me unravel completely. I can't even bring myself to moan, too lost in the feeling of them to know which way is up and which is down.

Clearly, my silence wasn't a good enough response because a thick finger rubs against my sensitive flesh, skyrocketing my desire. I scream out Letum's name as an onslaught of pleasure rips through my body, and I keep screaming as they fuck me ruthlessly, completely forgetting about the fact that I have neighbors.

"You're so beautiful," Letum purrs as they slam into me, increasing their speed. "Your body is mine." With a vicious thrust, Letum roars, spilling his seed into me. I try to focus on his soul and whether he spilled into me as well. While Letum softens inside of me, his soul remains completely hard.

Exhaustion weighs my limbs as I try to keep upright and stop my body from spasming as my orgasm fades away.

Letum and the soul pull out of me slowly, and I whimper at the profound emptiness. All the lights in my apartment turn off, blanketing the room in complete darkness so that I can only make out Letum's silhouette.

His soul's monstrous hands wrap around my hips and ease me onto the bed next to him, and the blankets immediately become damp with my sweat and wet hair.

The bed tips for a second, and I can only assume that Letum's soul is returning to his body. A wet cloth appears out of nowhere, and he wipes me down with it, taking extra care between my legs and my backside, then pats me dry with another towel.

Without really thinking anything through, I let him move me around like a puppet. Pulling my underwear up my legs because he seems to know that I hate being without it. Then he gets me to sit up so he can pull my arms through the holes of a fluffy robe that I'm certain I don't own. A comb seems to appear in his hand, and he brushes the wet hair off my face like I do after every shower.

Everything he's done from the shower to tucking me into bed with him pressed against my back made me forget about the pain of the last three weeks. The loneliness. The abandonment. Now it hits me like lightning, and I can think of nothing else.

"You left me," I whisper when the silence becomes as heavy as the weight on my chest.

"It destroyed me to do so, my love," he says against my hair. My heart aches for him, just as it does for me. I know that it was a necessary evil. "You still need more time."

My eyes burn, and a single tear falls onto the pillow. Being so emotional is much more taxing than being a medicated zombie.

"You're leaving me again?" My words come out stuttered and weak. I don't want him to know how much I missed him—how much I miss him even though he's right there—but the fact that he returns the sentiment and suffers like I am makes me feel slightly better.

"Not tonight." He hugs me tighter, and I wrap my hands around his arm reassuring myself that he's real. "Tonight, it's just you and me. I'm so proud of you, my love. You have come so far."

For once, I can't help thinking that I'm proud of myself too.

CHAPTER TWELVE

LILITH

I was hoping that Letum lied to me and he wouldn't leave me like he said he would. It was wishful thinking, but as far as I can tell, he has never told me a single lie.

It has been three months since I've seen him. However, I wake up every day and find a flower lying on the pillow next to me. It's a different type of the same flower each time: Asiatic lily, oriental lily, calla lily, daylily, madonna lily, tiger lily. I must say I've become an expert on all things lilies now, and I try to keep each flower alive as long as possible. I would much rather find him next to me or at least a note. I miss seeing his cursive writing and the combination of fear and excitement that hits me whenever I'd see one of his letters.

He's letting me travel this path alone, but he's constantly reminding me that he's a step behind me to stop me from falling over the edge of the cliff. Only now, his form of support isn't just solely emotional.

He may be death, but he's doing a lot to keep me alive.

A month ago, one of the floorboards lifted, and I kept tripping over it. Then, one day it was like it never even happened. Two weeks ago, I had some kind of infection, so Letum left antibiotics. Three days ago, I drove to work on a flat tire because I couldn't afford to miss my shift. After work, I found the wheel as good as new. The kitchen stool with the missing screw can now be safely sat on without risk of injury. Not to mention that the damage caused to my bathroom was repaired when I woke up in an empty bed the next day.

I've been back to see Dahlia and my parents almost every day. It's rather depressing that my closest friend is a corpse that can't talk back. Still, I like to imagine she's there sitting next to me, judging me, but loving me all the same.

I even visited Evan's gravesite. Though I didn't have many words for him, except the three that mattered: *I forgive you.*

I used to think that I was sorry, that I should have apologized to him for the situation we ended up in.

If Letum taught me anything, it is that there are two people in almost every relationship. Even if they're polar opposites, it'll work if they truly want it to work.

Maybe Evan did want it to work. Maybe I did too. We were so caught up in trying to pick up our own broken pieces that we didn't realize some of our shards were in the other person's hands. But everytime we shatter, we're bound to lose pieces. We forgot that we'd worked faster if we put the pieces back together as a team. Instead, Letum has been the one nudging me whenever a piece has gone astray. He's the one keeping me afloat on a sinking ship.

This time, I'll do what's right and put in the effort.

I pull my phone out of my bag—my *new* bag from Letum—then close my locker behind me and begin to type.

Me: I had a thought today (surprising, I know). If I had to guess, you'd order a short black coffee. And every few weeks you'll add sugar just to keep things interesting.

Me: Also, I'm not sure if you saw it this morning. I drove past a border collie that looked exactly like the puppy I had as a teenager. He had two different colored eyes, one black, and one blue. Rafe never listened to any order unless you had a treat.

Our message thread is full of green bubbles and not a single gray response. It seems like all my communications nowadays are one-sided and are related to the dead.

Brit pulls the chair out and slumps down onto it, defeat written all over her. The cafe has been understaffed for the past two weeks with practically everyone out sick. So we've both been working extra hours, which is good, because it means I don't need to rely on Letum leaving me cash in my bag—though it hasn't stopped him from spoiling me.

"Christ," she groans. "I'm going to need to see a fucking chiropractor for all the weight I'm pulling here."

I huff, and my lips pull up in a half smile. "Ask the big boss instead. He seems to be good at walking all over you."

She gasps. "Lili! Did you just use humor?"

I almost slipped into an easy grin. "It's payment for having an open bar last night."

Letum's rather aggressive shove to get me onto my feet was like getting water poured on my face to wake up in the morning: it feels like shit, but you're definitely awake now.

I've stopped mourning the girl that I once was and everything in my life that came before the accident. I won't say I've healed, but I'm on the path to recovery, and I think that's what really matters.

Hell, I even left my house to socialize last night for the first time in almost two years. It's a milestone, even if all I did was sit there and listen to everyone else talk.

Even after everything, I still can't shake the feeling that I'm missing something. Someone. I happened to text Letum in great detail about last night after I had one too many glasses of wine. Not much of my message was comprehensible, but he must have understood what I was saying because when I got home there was a sandwich on the counter, toothpaste on my toothbrush, a glass of water next to my bed, and an extra lily on my pillow.

I'm trying to remind myself that actions speak louder than words, but it's hard to think that when I haven't heard a single word from him.

Even though life is finally shaping up, it doesn't feel like this is the right life for me. I'm not just meaning life in a cafe or this city. Something deeper and more intrinsic that I don't have the necessary words to explain.

"Honestly, I don't know how you're even upright today," Brit grumbles.

The truth is, I've had a little more energy every day. I'm not sure if I can owe it to the lack of medication or the fact that I'm not crying myself to sleep anymore.

"I stayed away from the tequila," I point out.

The door to the cafe swings open, and my coworker sticks his head around with a frantic yet unimpressed look. "Brit, there's a lady that wants to *speak* to you about the taste of her scone."

She groans into her hands and looks up at me with her bloodshot eyes. "If you hear screaming, don't call the police."

I nod and grin. "Noted."

CHAPTER THIRTEEN
LILITH

I GRAB MY PHONE as I walk to my apartment the next day and see the last two texts that I sent him during my lunch break, still unanswered.

> **Me:** There's a candlelit piano concert coming to town that I think you might like.

> **Me:** I saw a dress online, and the concert would be the perfect occasion to wear it. I'm just not sure whether to get it in forest green or sage green.

Maybe it is a bit pathetic that I'm texting someone who isn't texting back, especially when the texts are so mundane. But it makes me feel like I'm connected to him, even though I'm certain he's still watching my every move.

> **Me:** I'm going to make
> spaghetti aglio e olio for din-
> ner if you'd like to join. I
> can't promise it will taste as
> good as what you make, but
> nothing is wrong with striv-
> ing for 'edible'.

I let out a half laugh as I sent the latest text. He's never taken me up on my offer but I haven't given up trying. Honestly, he probably already knows that I am going to make the dish when I bought all of the ingredients for it yesterday.

I haven't stopped trying to coax him out of the shadows. I've walked around my apartment practically naked, used his money to buy lingerie, put on a good show with my fingers, and moaned his name for added effect in the hopes that maybe he'll take me by surprise again.

One might say I've gone to extreme lengths in my desperation.

Still, he hasn't so much as left me a letter. I'm disappointed, to say the least. And sad. I miss him.

> **Me:** And we can watch
> Ghost Rider after dinner,

> then you can tell me whether
> it's fact or fiction.

My heart skips a beat when my phone vibrates in my hand.

> **Letum:** Fiction.

The smile that spreads on my face stretches from ear to ear. After three months, he responds with a single word. *Finally.*

Childlike giddiness fills me from seeing his name on the screen. I have no control over the butterflies that spur alive in my stomach.

> **Me:** It's fact until you come
> over to convince me that it's
> fiction.

> **Letum:** Soon, my Lilith.

The weirdest part about the past month is that with each passing day, I feel closer to Letum. Not physically, of course. And not because I've realized the method to his madness. But because in the back of my mind, bits and pieces of information are sitting beneath the surface of rippling water, and occasionally, I can see what it says.

For some reason, I can say with utter confidence that Letum has raven black hair and eyes of plain white. Just as I can confidently say that he has a dimple on his chin, thick curling lashes, and a short horizontal scar on his cheek. I'm not sure how I might know this, but I would bet everything that I have ever known on these simple facts.

I make enough dinner for two. To no one's surprise, he doesn't show. Does death eat (something other than me)? Probably not.

He shouldn't have responded to my text, because all it did was make me yearn for him even more. His touch, his voice, his taste.

The wooden floor is a welcome discomfort as I sit in front of the drawers in my bedroom. The last time I opened the drawer with all his notes and extra gifts was three months ago.

A pink lily looks down at me from my desk, perched on a glass. *Stargazer*, botanists call it. Out of all the kinds of lilies that he's brought me, the Stargazer is my favorite. Its hot pink spots lighten my otherwise dull room. The vibrant color is the complete opposite of both Letum and me. It's meant to symbolize prosperity and abundance.

All the lilies have found a home somewhere around my apartment. If they aren't hanging onto life soaking up some water, then they're hanging on a string upside down. Just because it's dead, it doesn't mean it can't be beautiful.

Too weak to hold it back, I grab my phone and send another text.

Me: I miss you, Letum.
'Soon' isn't soon enough.

I stare at the green bubble, waiting to see more gray ones pop up, but nothing comes.

Sighing, I try to bite down my disappointment. Two texts don't mean that he's coming. Neither does two lilies.

I wrap my fingers around the metal handle of the drawer and try to pull it open. When it doesn't budge I use far more force than necessary, and the whole drawer lands on my lap, spilling brown parchment all over the floor.

I blink.

I blink again.

The whole thing is filled to the brim with rolled-up brown parchment. It's no longer kept together tidily in a box. Rolls of paper fall into the box of feathers, and make their way into every nook and cranny of the drawer.

I grab the first letter I can get my hands on and read it with bated breath.

You make me feel alive.

It's new. It's a new letter. He's never said that to me before.

I reach for another one.

Get the dress in forest green. It compliments your skin tone. Though there is nothing you could wear that wouldn't take my breath away.

The corners of my lips tip up and a deep blush taints my cheeks. This entire time I thought he was trying to keep his distance and ignore me.

> *Seeing as you have been telling me about your day, I shall tell you about mine.*

> *Today I watched the most otherworldly soul smile as she gazed upon a flower. Though my heart is greedy because I only want her to smile for me.*

Stupid tears well in my eyes. I wipe it away before it can fall onto the paper, and I grab another letter.

> *Heaven does not compare to your beauty.*

Then another letter.

> *Every day I watch you grow, and I could not be prouder.*

And another.

> *You are almost there, my love. A while longer, and we will have an eternity together.*

Then another.

> *You're right. If I drank coffee, I would have a short*
> *black.*

One by one, I unroll the letters and try to wipe away the tears before they fall. I feel like I can't breathe, not because it hurts but because this is what I've been missing. *He* is what I have been missing.

This whole time I thought the accident was the worst thing that could have happened to me and that nothing good could ever come from it. But deep down, I knew—I really always knew—I belonged to death. The world of the living isn't meant for me. Despite the life I led before the accident, I didn't truly feel alive. Something was always off.

A tuft of black catches my eye from within the drawer, hidden beneath the mounds of parchment. I fish through the letters until my fingers wrap around something soft and fluffy.

A sob escapes my lips when I pull it out and stare into the different colored eyes of the stuffed animal. Black fur and white socks, and an asymmetrical pool of white going from its neck, down to its stomach. *Rafe.* Letum made a toy dog that looks exactly like my old boy.

This time, when the tears fall, I don't stop them. I shove my face into the animal and pour my eyes out.

What did I do to deserve Letum's attention? How is it that the most thoughtful, caring, and attentive person that I have ever met is death itself?

Something soft hits my head. I suck in a breath and snap my gaze away from Rafe in time to watch a letter tumble down my shoulder.

My heart hammers in my chest with an intoxicating mix of excitement and nerves as I unwrap the letter.

If soon cannot come soon enough, then come find me, my night monster.

I will give you a hint: To end, you must go to the beginning.

I frown. What does he mean? Is he finally going to let me see him? What does he mean by 'the beginning'? I was born in the hospital two towns over, but a hospital isn't the most romantic of places to meet. Though I guess it would be easier for him if he's collecting souls.

Also, what am I ending? He can't possibly mean ending our relationship.

As I stare at the letter, the realization hits me. I know where to find him. I pull my phone out and send him words that he's said to me.

Me: I'm coming for you.

My feet fly down the stairs as I run to my car. I'm barely breathing. Barely thinking rationally. I'm blinded by thoughts of him. He's finally letting me see him. *Finally*.

The city lights disappear as I get on the road that leads out into the forest. The moon is nowhere to be seen, hidden beneath fields of vicious clouds.

This whole time he was getting me to face my past and move beyond the things that were holding me back. He got rid of Evan, not for laying a hand on me, but because he was holding me back. Death left me letters not just to keep me standing, but to get my legs to move me forward.

Beneath my ribs, my heart rattles and sings with anticipation and fear and excitement. I've avoided this road since the accident, refusing to drive to Evan's parent's house just because this whole street is haunted by memories of that night. Yet, here I am, speeding toward it.

Maybe I'm not ready to face this place. I don't think I'll ever be. But I am beyond ready to drive past it.

I slow down and anxious critters crawl up my neck as I near the site that burned my sister alive. I immediately grab hold of the necklace to remind myself that Letum will be there.

The tree looks so innocent, standing on the side of a sharp bend in the road. No one would know that it's a killer. Though, I suppose the bystander is the one that holds the blame, not the tree that is just trying to live.

I pull over to the side of the road, leaving my headlights directed straight at the tree and the hooded man standing in front of it.

For one second, everything stops. The world around me doesn't exist except for him. Then everything flies by as I run toward him, trampling over grass and fallen leaves.

He doesn't move a muscle as I stand before him, holding my breath so he doesn't hear me pant. My entire being freezes when I look into the space beneath his hood. A dimpled chin. Soft, supple lips. A lethally edged jaw. High cheekbones. All are shadowed beneath the hood but illuminated by the headlights.

I hold my breath as I reach out for his hood. For the first time, he doesn't stop me when I trail my fingers along the soft cotton edge of his hoodie. I pull the material off his face and almost stagger back from his beauty. He's exactly as I thought he looked, raven colored hair and thick black lashes fanning over his pupiless white eyes that see everything.

My heart seems to slow, and everything comes rushing back to me, overloading my senses so much that I almost buckle over. I know him. I know him like the back of my hand. Almost every night, he would help me escape, pulling me into the space between dreams to talk. His bedroom, the forest, the beach; I've been to all of them a hundred times before. I've gazed into his eyes a thousand times before, and it makes me melt every time.

Tears stream down my cheek as I drink him in. He's the most beautiful thing I've ever seen. I think about it every time he let me see his face.

I remember now. I remember every single time we've sat on the beach to watch the storm, while he told me tales of the world that has gone by. Every time he had me perched on his bed as he read me sonnets and stories. Every time he looked at me like nothing else mattered except the words that came out of my mouth.

I was another person in those dreams, yet I was the same. That Lili held all of the memories of the nights before, all of the sweet words whispered by Death. She knew that upon waking, I would forget all about the dreams. I wish I had never forgotten about him, but I'll never forget again.

I forgot all about Death because of Dr. Mallory's medication and the wound on my heart that refused to heal. Now that I remember Death, I would spend an eternity committing every word to memory and still be starved for more.

"Now you see, my night monster."

I nod. *His* love. I am his; I always was, I just didn't know it. He may not have taken my soul the night of the accident, but he did claim it. My body and soul stopped being mine the second I saw him. He's the only one who has ever truly understood me; the loneliness, the call for the darkness, watching everyone I cared about die.

Without thinking, I stand on the tips of my toes and wrap my arms around his neck to bask in the smell that has been imprinted on my soul. His lips press against mine and our kiss is filled with so many firsts, and no lasts. The kiss is a promise of forever. Forever remembering every forgotten word. Forever relishing in every touch. Forever with *Death*.

"Thank you," I whisper against his lips. "Thank you for waiting for me. Thank you for helping me see who I am."

He kisses me with the weight of a thousand strikes of lightning. "Always, my love."

"I'm ready."

He frowns.

"I want you, Death. I want all of you. I see it now. I see the truth," I say. He wipes the tears from my cheek, staring down at me intensely with his forehead resting against my own. "You were made for me, just as I was made for you. You complete me, Letum." I kiss him to try and convey everything I'm saying so he knows without a sliver of doubt that I am telling the truth. "I give you my soul. For the rest of eternity, it is yours. Even in death, I am yours."

He doesn't say anything for a moment, and my heart falls to my feet. But the feeling is fleeting because he yearns for me just as much as I do for him.

The first drop of rain hits my cheeks, then more droplets splatter against our skin, soaking our clothes.

"You, my love, are like a storm, drowning the land with sorrow, shattering ships with your broken waves. Still, you look into the eye of the storm and see nothing but beauty." He pulls my head to the side and dips down so his lips are against my ear. "Let me drown in your ocean and feel your rage. Let me feel your waves crash against my skin, pulling me deeper into your depths so you will never be alone again." His thumb grazes my lip before he claims me completely with a kiss. "You are the sunrise after the storm. The new beginning and the dawn. You, my flower, are beauty personified."

"I love you, Letum." I've said it before, in a dream.

How it hurts to say those three words and not remember them when you wake. But I know them to be truer than my own name.

He smiles, and I try to capture the image in my mind to save it and look at it whenever I'd like. "Oh, my Lilith. I love you more than the moon longs for the sun."

We stand like that, holding each other, memorizing the moment. "I'm ready," I say once more.

"Are you sure? There is no going back."

I nod and pull out of his touch to lower myself to the ground. I've never been more sure of anything in my life.

He gets down onto his knees next to me, and I give him a reassuring nod. The sky flashes with bright light, and a bolt of lightning torments the ground nearby. Thunder booms through the windy road and the surrounding trees.

When Death's lips touch mine, every bit of pain I've ever held disappears. There's no anger, no grief, no sorrow. Only the understanding that everything is the way it should be. Everything is washed away with the sea, and all that's left is... *contentment*.

In that moment, everything that has happened in my life flashes before my eyes. Dahlia and I blowing out candles on our flower shaped birthday cake. Tripping as I walk onto the stage to receive my bachelors. Going shopping with mom to pick out clothes for my dream interview. Dad handing me the keys to my first car. Evan and I camped out in his car beside the river, eating unsavory amounts of cheese and crackers. All of those beautiful moments in time that never felt complete.

Not like it does now.

Letum helps me to my feet and entwines our fingers. I look down, and my own lifeless body gets trampled by the rain, but I feel nothing. Lightning strikes once more, illuminating my peaceful expression.

He cups my jaw and brings me to face him. "To eternity together."

"And in death afterward," I whisper back.

The scenery around us flickers with lights from another car. Tires screech along the street, and we both turn to watch the car spin as it takes the sharp turn, tipping onto its roof before it hits the same tree that killed my sister and her boyfriend with a violent crash.

Something from the car tugs at the empty space in my chest. I look at Letum in question. He squeezes my hand and lets it go, giving me a subtle nod.

Next to the car, a big luminescent cloud of light dances and spins in the air. Soft voices come from behind it, calling and beckoning. Not for me, but for the soul in the car. I'm not sure how I know, but it's a gateway. The same gateway Death did not want to take me to.

I breathe in deeply, then follow the pull. Everything about this feels like I'm finally breathing fresh air. It feels right. The broken glass beneath my feet doesn't make a sound as I make my way to the car. My knees don't click when I drop to my haunches to see inside the car.

Through the shattered window, I can see a boy with red hair hanging upside down in his seat with his spine jutting out of the side of his neck, beneath his skin.

I look back at Death, the once faceless man, whose face is now all I see. Letum gives me a reassuring nod. My attention goes back to the boy with the red hair: the soul that isn't mine to keep.

Thunder rolls through the hills as the rain falls harder, soaking the earth and my lifeless body. The gates vibrate the world around, and the pull grows stronger.

This is what I was always meant to do. This is what I was made for. Letum is who I was made for.

Death comes in the darkness and light, but for him, I will come in a storm.

The End.

ACKNOWLEDGMENTS

I HAD A FEW people ask me what inspired this book.

The answer comes down to several things:

1. I wanted a freaky little man to leave me concerning notes while I slept.

2. Shadow daddies are hot.

3. Lilith is hot.

4. Untreated ADHD.

5. I was driving and *Freefall* was playing by Rainbow Kitten Surprises, and the following words spoke to me on a near spiritual level:

Called to the Devil and the Devil said Hey!
Why you been calling this late?
It's like 2 A.M. and the bars all close at 10 in hell, that's
a rule I made
Anyway, you say you're too busy saving everybody else to

save yourself
And you don't want no help, oh well
That's the story to tell

But aside from that, I want to thank my amazing team of beta readers: V, Sam, Kiza, Pia, Nadine, Jacki, Kayla, Mika, Mette, Ruby, Nildene, and Nika (and for the stunning drawing of the skull). If I could, I would put a very specific emoji next to each of your names, but unfortunately that would be a nightmare to figure out from a typesetting perspective. But honestly, this book wouldn't be where it is without you all, baby girls.

A special shout out to V, Sam and Kiza for your unwavering support from an emotional, spiritual and physical perspective. I love you guys.

About the Author

From an early age, romance author Avina St. Graves spent her days imaging fantasy worlds and dreamy fictional men, which spurred on from her introverted tendencies. In all her day dreaming, there seemed to be a reoccurring theme of morally grey female characters, love interests that belong in prison, and unnecessary trauma and bloodshed.

Much to everyone's misfortune, she now spends her days in a white-collar job praying to every god known to man that she might be able to write full time and give the world more red flags to froth over. Follow her on Instagram, Facebook and Tiktok.

Made in the USA
Monee, IL
03 July 2024

61170999R00104